The Deeper Dark

By Michael Allen

Copyright © 2020 Michael Allen

All rights reserved. No part of this book may be reproduced in any form by any electronic or mechanical means, including information storage and retrieval systems, without permission in writing from the author, except by a reviewer who may quote brief passages in a review.

ISBN 979-8574359709

Michael Allen

Michaelallenonline.com

Dedication

To the two most important people in my life, my daughter and my mother…

Mikayla,

You have become the most amazing lady. I love everything about you, especially your strength. I hope you know how much you mean to me and that I love you.

Mom,

You did an outstanding job raising me and now, you're more of a friend. We can talk about anything and you are truly an inspiration for everything I do. I'm quite sure you already know how much I love you!

Table of Contents

Chapter I	1
Chapter II	19
Chapter III	43
Chapter IV	59
Chapter V	73
Chapter VI	89
Chapter VII	105
Chapter VIII	125
Chapter IX	139
Chapter X	153
Chapter XI	169
Chapter XII	181
Chapter XIII	191
Chapter XIV	205
Chapter XV	219
Chapter XVI	227
Chapter XVII	237

Chapter I

"When the world is screaming in your ears, you have to be your own peace."

They knocked on the door like cops who were coming to make an arrest. They knocked at random times throughout the night to wake up the prisoners and keep them from getting used to any sort of pattern. Their tactics jarred a prisoner's psyche and dug deep under his nerves so that every moment he spent in their cages was on the edge of a total breakdown. That is if they could get him to finally break down.

Haven Kayd had been on a mission years ago to fly over the area and gather intel with the digital recording equipment installed underneath his fighter jet, a jet also equipped with enough firepower to level a compound if the mission called for it. But the Captain experienced equipment failure that brought his jet down right in the middle of enemy territory. He was able to land instead of jettisoning, but the landing was far from smooth and it attracted a lot of attention.

The next thing he knew, there were AK-47s pointed at his face from all different directions. Ironically, those were the same AK-47s America had supplied the Afghans back in the 80s. Isn't it interesting how small details like that jump up to bite us in the end?

They covered his head and made him walk miles with his hands tied to ropes attached to his feet. When they finally stepped foot on the compound, they took his flight gear and his boots. One guerilla wrote his name on a shirt they gave him while another recorded it in a logbook. Then, they threw him in a cell with nothing but a drain in the middle of the floor that emitted the odor of old urine from hundreds of prisoners who had been there before him.

Tired, he took a seat on the floor, and just as his eyes started to feel the heavy weight of exhaustion, he felt the shock shoot through his body of the prison guard pounding on the steel door. Just as his mind was about to shut down and allow him to escape the miserable existence he presently found himself in, the pounding on the door would instantly bring him back to his concrete walls and that sharp smell of urine. This had become his reality.

Of course, during the day, there was plenty for him to do. He was escorted to different parts of the compound for various reasons. He was interrogated in one room, and then recorded in another as proof of custody. America seemed interested in saving him, but Haven knew their policy. They were pretty set on not negotiating with terrorists. He was making his peace with the fact that he just might never see home again.

Those were the images that filled his mind whenever he had downtime. He would think of his daughter's cute smile and when his mind wandered, he could almost feel her hand in his again. She would sit on his lap after a long day and tell him all kinds of stories while his wife sat on the couch laughing at all the detail his little princess muttered through. That's when Haven would stop himself from thinking, from remembering. He couldn't afford to think about those times. He had to break his mind free from wanting to be back there, from wanting to ever see them again.

Days became months and months blended into a long blurry string of time. Haven had no idea what year it was. He had missed so many birthdays, he had no idea how big Lara had gotten. His marriage, his small family was nothing but a faded memory now. He had struggled with his will to survive and it had won every time. Committing suicide simply wasn't an option. But if they killed him, that would certainly do the trick. That would be very merciful, and it would finally end the misery.

In the time he had spent in the POW camp, Haven had picked up on a few things. He knew the guerillas had some patience and could wait out a president. If Haven wasn't going to be an effective bargaining chip for them under one administration, they could wait until another won the seat. But that was it. They didn't have too much patience after that.

Without having access to news and having only picked up on a little Persian, Haven wasn't absolutely sure of what was going on around him. But he could feel the climate and he knew his days were limited. He had watched a few prisoners get escorted out to never return. His was just a matter of time.

He hadn't confessed to anything and he hadn't fallen for any of their ploys to trick him into saying something controversial on camera. So, he knew he was of no more value to them at all. When he took itinerary of himself, his situation became even more dire. He had no shoes, and his clothes were hand-me-downs from dead prisoners. The guerillas didn't even take the time to wash the holy threads before throwing them in Haven's cell. With very little choice, he put them on reluctantly and that was all he had to his name.

If he was going to try to fight his way out of the compound, it was going to be the most useless attempt. But he was determined that was going to be his way. Where they were planning on taking him was a walk to his gruesome death anyway. He knew the guerillas weren't nice about it either. They liked cutting throats with machetes. Sometimes, they would stone a prisoner to death. Either way, Haven was sentenced to die. He figured he might as well put up a fight so that if the truth ever got out about him, that story would be his legacy.

It was easy for days to blend into each other. The lights stayed on all the time and there were no windows to tell the night from day. But something had changed. Haven wasn't sure what it was, but he could tell. There was something different and it was definitely noticeable.

From his cell of three concrete walls and a steel door mostly covering the fourth wall, he had limited access to other prisoners and he could barely see through the cracks around the door. But he knew something was amiss. One day, there was less activity. The prison guards weren't walking the hallway as much. They had stopped banging on the doors at all hours of the night.

It had been a long time, but Haven finally got a few hours of uninterrupted sleep. His mind was able to totally shut down and the exhaustion completely melted away. When he woke up after what felt like forever, his groggy mind couldn't quite put it together right away, but something felt odd. When his mind started to clear, he could feel he was a little colder than usual and another small detail struck him. He realized the lights were off.

"How long was I asleep," he thought as his soul suddenly shook with dread. His mind began to race as the reality of his new situation started to set in. He was no longer a prisoner because there was no longer an enemy holding him captive. The bad part was he had been abandoned and left to rot in a locked cage.

Sure, he may have made peace with them killing him, but he hadn't made peace with this turn of events. He hadn't even attempted to fathom a scenario in which he was left behind in a small cage in the middle of nowhere. He had gotten used to not eating. The guerillas hadn't been too consistent about feeding the prisoners and they hadn't been very generous with their portions either. But if Haven had known that his last meal was actually going to be his last meal, he might have tried to savor it.

Getting shot or stabbed was one thing but dying a slow death without food and water was just more misery than he could handle. In his desperation, he started to shake the door knowing it wouldn't magically come open just like the other thousands of times he had tried. When his aggravation ran out, he tried to be more logical about getting out.

Metal bolts held the metal frame to the concrete wall surrounding it. The concrete wall had little give, but Haven did notice a crack that he might be able to work into an opening. He could only hope it wouldn't take long. But rather than dive into that solution, he thought he'd look for an easier way if one existed.

"What shape is the lock in," he asked himself as he started to feel around the doorframe where the lock mechanism was. The only light coming in was from the sun shining through some opening on the other side of Haven's door. One thing he noticed about it was that it was slowly starting to fade. That was the first time he had been able to tell that it was day and night was coming soon.

He had no idea what to expect. He fumbled with the lock for as long as he could see, but night soon came and that's when he felt the cold fall on the cell. By morning, it had set into the core of his bones. His shattering teeth woke him up and his shivering body was out of control. It took the heat of the sun beating on the roof above him hours later to finally take off the chill.

His hands stiff and cramped, he did his best to figure out the locking mechanism. He noticed some give and as he played around with it, he also saw that there was a latch on the outside. He was on the wrong side of the door to be able to do anything with it. That's when the crack in the concrete again suddenly became the more feasible option.

He pushed on the wall and then wrapped his fingers around the edge to pull on it. He pushed a few times in a row and then pulled a few times more. He became more and more frantic with every push and pull but he didn't let himself lose heart even though the task seemed useless.

He looked around the cell in desperation and then returned to his work on the crack in the concrete. Once in a while, he would put his head down in defeat. Then, he would shake it off and draw in a deep breath. Back to pushing and pulling with no idea if it was even working but he was determined that faith was going to get him through, or he was going to die in that lonely cell.

When night came, the cold set in again and even though Haven tried to keep going, his fingers stiffened and the miserable shiver took over his body once more. Night and day, night and day again, he kept working. He started to believe in what he was doing when he noticed the crack actually getting bigger and concrete debris piling up below him.

After a few miserable days, he noticed the doorframe start to move slightly. His work was becoming more and more effective. He fought with the hunger pangs that would come and go. He fought with his headache and the pain that had set in throughout his body. He was starting to feel the taste of freedom and he was more determined than ever to get out.

Finally, a part of the wall fell away, exposing a bolt. That bolt became his lifesaver. He worked on it, pushing it up and down, pulling it in toward him and then working it out against the concrete wall. He worked it until the head of the bolt broke off. That was when he had his first tool and he used it to dig through the broken concrete. It was easier with a piece of metal than with his fingers. As more concrete debris piled up below him, he gained more faith that he would get out of his forgotten cell.

When a hole formed, he started digging more frantically. The hole that started small was soon big enough for his arm to fit through and after feeling around the latch to figure out how the moving parts worked, he was free. The steel door swung open and out stepped a man of skin and bones. Standing with no shoes and in shredded clothes, Haven didn't have time to worry about the fact that he was not equipped to face the extreme conditions on the outside of those walls.

When Haven looked around, he realized that he had been locked up in a makeshift prison with very little security measures beyond his cell. He followed the light to find his way out of the small building where the prisoners had been housed. That's when he felt a sharp pain shoot through him. Walking on rocks barefoot reminded him that he needed to find something to protect his feet.

The compound was empty as if it had been disserted a long time ago. His sense of time was off, but he was sure it hadn't been that long. He looked all around the compound and found very little to work with. When the guerillas abandoned the place, they took everything they could carry. But Haven was able to find some cloth to wrap around his feet and give them some protection. He was also able to find some running water, which he gulped uncontrollably until he couldn't breathe. Then, he rested a second and drank some more.

When he got his fill of water, he tried to put all the pieces of the puzzle together from his mission a few years ago. He could see a partial map in his mind. It wasn't the best memory, but what he remembered was going to have to do. The more he thought about everything, the more he recalled the direction he was going those many years ago and his destination. All he needed was to try to recall everything he could about the Afghanistan countryside.

If he went in the right direction, he could find a river that flowed by woodland. If he went the wrong way, he'd be walking through miles of desert. His thirst for water was the only thing holding him from going. He couldn't get enough even though he knew it wasn't good to drink himself sick. He just didn't know how far he was going to have to go until he saw water again, so his fear was overriding his logic until he was able to finally pull himself away.

When he stepped out of the compound, he looked around to see if he could acclimate himself to any memory he had of the area. Of course, the wooded area he spotted to his left seemed to be the reasonable way to go. Sweating and dragging his feet, he made it to the woodline where he took a seat and rested for a moment in the shade. His hands were shaking and his body was paying the toll but he had to keep going. He had to push himself to keep going.

Every time he took a break, it was harder and harder for him to get going again. The breaks were coming too frequently and they were lasting longer. But something seemed familiar in the way he was going.

When he found water again, he dipped his face in it and splashed it all over him. It felt great against the hot sun beating down on him all day. The water looked crystal clear, probably better than the running water in the compound. So, he drank as much as he could before heading out again.

He stayed in the shade as much as possible. Even though it wasn't much cooler in there, it beat the direct heat that stung his skin. It made movement easier and when he took his mind off of all the pain he was feeling throughout his body from his bloody feet to his empty stomach that felt like it was eating itself, he could make good time even though his blurry vision and the slight dizziness in his head was a good indication he was about to fall out.

He picked a spot by the water and dug himself a small hole in the sand. Then, he used his Boy Scout training the Marines had taught him to start a fire in the hole that wouldn't be detected at night. He built himself a small wall about a foot high with sticks to reflect the heat back his way where he had gathered some foliage to cover himself. He was surprised to learn that nights in this climate didn't drop as low as he had previously thought. His nights in his cell had tricked his mind into believing he was about to go through a potentially fatal freeze-over.

As soon as he covered himself with the foliage he had found, his eyes grew heavy and his mind wandered off into images of his daughter and his wife. This time, he didn't fight it. He allowed himself to dream. He actually had hope again and with that, he could allow himself to want those things once more. He could allow himself to fight to get his life back. His daughter's smile and endless tales, his wife's laugh and adoring look of admiration made him sleep in peace for several hours.

He woke up a new man even though his stomach was still empty and crying out in hunger pangs, his body still aching and screaming for more rest. But his mind was refreshed and his faith renewed. He was going to go home again. He could taste it.

It was still dark when he woke up. He kicked dirt into his fire hole and headed East, the direction he had been going since leaving the compound. It felt right to go East. Even though it had been years, his gut instinct was telling him he was going in the right direction. And before long, it was confirmed. The miles he had been forced to walk those several years before were the same miles he had just walked again. There in front of him was his old jet.

The Deeper Dark

It had been stripped down to the bone. The guerillas had taken all the missiles and firepower the jet could hold. But they had left some very important things behind. Haven climbed up into the cockpit and looked around. He knew that jet like the back of his hand. The equipment was still there and if there was any hope in this dire situation at all, he'd find the one thing he desperately needed the most.

Stowed behind the seat was the solar-powered radio that would save his life. It powered up without a problem. It sure beat the hand crank dinosaurs the military had used for the longest time. A sigh of relief escaped his lips as he slid down in the seat like a baby with the radio tucked in his arms like a Teddy Bear. Tears started in his eyes as he looked at the radio and then looked around. He started laughing but it was a laugh that was shared with tears.

Chapter II

"Bad times are just an illusion for the good times to show their face."

"Lara! Are you ready yet," Monica yelled up the steps as she rummaged through her pocketbook and checked her look in the mirror. With blonde hair and piercing blue eyes, Monica was a stunning lady decked out in designer jeans and high heels. Her white crop top made her tan look as if she glowed in the dark. She was a very refined lady with not a hair out of place.

"We don't need to rush," Skip said in jest as he walked by her and kissed her on the neck. Skip was also a well-dressed man with a very distinguished look. His dark hair and tall physique made them look like the perfect couple.

She turned to him and put her hand to his face, "You know how I am. I have to be ready to go early so that we can show up fashionably late." She smiled and kissed him on his lips.

"That's one of those quirks that get me about you," Skip answered as he looked up the steps.

Lara was finally ready and she was making her entrance. Skip nodded with a smile on his face as he watched Lara come down the stairs. Her long brown hair flowed over her shoulders and accentuated her green eyes.

"There you are baby," Monica put her hands to her mouth as a tear came to her eyes.

"Mom, I'm not a baby anymore," Lara protested.

"You'll always be my baby," Monica quickly corrected.

"Are you ready for your big day," Skip asked with an adoring look at the little lady standing in front of him.

"I think so," Lara answered. She was thirteen and she was getting ready to graduate Junior High. It was a big deal for her because she had struggled with school most of her life. All she knew was that her father had died on a mission. Even learning about it at a young age, it was hard for her to handle. Each year getting harder and harder. She was just starting to get over it and move past the pain.

Making it through the eighth grade was quite an achievement. Skip and Monica had been pulling extra hard for her to simply get through each grade year after year. But now, she would be leaving Junior High and going to High School. It was a very special day.

Monica gave her a huge hug and then, she stood back from her daughter so that she could study her face while she ran her fingers through her hair. Lara had the saddest eyes even though her face was trying to smile. Monica could see the sadness and if she could do anything, she'd take it all away. She would just have to do it one hug at a time.

That's when they heard the knock on the door. They looked around at each other with curious looks on their faces. Who would be coming to their house at this time in the morning? Who was getting company just before the Junior High graduation?

Skip answered the door to find two Marines dressed in uniform, "Can I help you?"

By then, Monica and Lara were at the door. The Marines looked at Monica and one of them asked, "Are you Monica Kayd?"

Monica hadn't heard that name for some time, "Um, I used to be. I'm Monica Webber now."

The Marine followed up, "Were you married to Captain Haven Kayd, ma'am?"

"Yes. Yes, I was. What is this about?"

"Mom, what's going on," Lara asked as she looked at her mother and then back at the Marines on her porch.

"Your husband has been located and is being transported to the States as we speak," the Marine started to inform.

"He's...he's alive," Monica interrupted. She put her hand to her heart and tears filled her eyes.

"Dad," Lara's heart filled with so much emotion, she let out the most heartbreaking sound as she realized who the Marine was talking about, "Dad's alive?"

Skip pulled his girls to him and wrapped his arms around them. The Marine continued to speak, but Monica and Lara weren't listening. Skip nodded as he heard what the Marine was saying. Someone had to keep it together so that they would know where to be and when they were going to get to see Haven again.

Monica and Lara were so full of emotion, they practically melted in Skip's arms. Then, Monica pulled herself away and stepped out onto the porch, "Captain Haven Kayd? You're sure? Because I've already gone through this once and I can't go through this again if you're not right."

The Marines nodded, "We're sure, ma'am. It's him. We positively identified him and other than some malnutrition and complications from dehydration, he's bouncing back from what he's been through."

"What he's been through," Monica asked.

The Marines looked at her and nodded. One cocked his head and tried to continue in an apologetic tone, "We can't go into any of that ma'am."

"You're going do that," Monica looked back and forth between both Marines, "You're going to pull that now?" Monica looked at Lara and put her arms out, "Come here, honey!"

Lara pulled herself away from Skip and went to her mother, "Mom, what are they saying?"

"I don't know honey," Monica answered, "Your father's alive. That's all we know right now." Monica stroked Lara's hair, "Your father's alive."

"Dad," Lara uttered through tears. Then, her body started to shake uncontrollably as she wept in her mother's arms.

§

Staring at the mirror above his dresser, Haven couldn't believe how much he had changed over the years. His eyes were sunk in and his jawbones were protruding. His teeth needed to be fixed and his body was skin and bones. The doctor told him he'd get his health back, but it was hard to imagine as he stood there looking at himself.

"What a mess," he thought but he was full of relief. A special forces team had been chosen to extract him and he was brought aboard the USS Peralta, which was the closest vessel in the area. He had received immediate medical treatment and then he was assigned a private room for a few days until further transport could be arranged.

Of course, the sailors aboard the Peralta were celebrating him. They applauded as he was helicoptered onto the ship and everyone wanted to meet him. The C.O. was making arrangements for a party with him as the guest of honor, but he had also ordered his sailors not to make too much of a fuss. Captain Kayd was to be allowed to rest until he got his strength back. Plus, he was to be given all the food The Captain desired.

Looking at the mirror in front of him, he wasn't just studying how much his looks had changed. He had slipped into deep thought about what he had just been through. He couldn't believe his room was real. He couldn't believe he was standing on a Naval vessel. He had resigned himself to die and to fight for his life while going down. But here he was, safe and sound with clean and dry clothes on his back, boots on his feet, and a bed to sleep on.

He looked up at the door when he heard the knock, "Yeah? Come in."

A cook popped his head through the door, "I thought you'd like a couple of cheeseburgers and some fries Captain."

"Oh," Haven's eyes grew wide with surprise, "That would be great. Yeah."

The cook brought the covered plate in and put it on the table. He pulled some packets of mustard and ketchup out of his pockets and then, he placed a can of cold Coke on the table, "If you need anything else, just ask. I got you, sir!"

"Oh man," Kayd looked at the burgers as he uncovered them, "This looks great. Thank you."

"No problem sir," the cook nodded and then headed toward the door, "I'll leave you to it."

"Hey uh," Haven started.

The cook turned around and looked back at the Captain, "Findley."

"Findley," Haven repeated, "Thanks for everything. I really do appreciate it."

Findley nodded, "After what you've been through sir, just snap your fingers if you want something. We've got you."

Haven nodded as his face twisted slightly with emotion. Findley was moved, but he tried his best not to show it.

"Okay then," Findley put his head down and closed the door behind him.

Haven looked around at the cheeseburgers with a kid's look of wonder in his eyes. He pulled the chair away from the table and took a seat. He had just eaten not more than an hour before but who could turn down a cheeseburger?

Halfway through his burger, Haven's subconscious stopped him for a moment. As he held the burger in his hand, his eyes locked on it as he slipped into deep thought once again. He was eating a burger! He was holding a burger in his hand! The reality of his situation hadn't quite caught up to him yet.

Just a few days before, he had been eating some slop out of a plate that he couldn't even identify. The food he was given in the compound took some getting used to and he wasn't quite sure it was even food most of the time. He was certain that the guerillas might have put some rat feces in it from time to time just for kicks. He knew they might have even spit in his food on occasion. What was in his food was up for anyone's imagination, but he ate it because there was nothing else.

Now, he was holding a warm cheeseburger in his hand. His mind kept playing tricks on him. Was this real? Or was he back in that cell imagining all this?

Another knock on the door shook him back to reality. He looked up at it, "Yeah? Come in."

That's when Haven saw a familiar face. His eyes lit up with excitement as he put his burger back on the plate and stood up to greet his old friend, "Stew! They let you on here?"

Stew came into the room with the biggest smile on his face. He was a solid man with a tall build and a tight buzz cut, "Well, they call me Colonel now. Rank has its privileges."

"Colonel," Haven repeated with a look of admiration, "How long have I been gone?"

"Yeah. It's been a few years Haven," Stew nodded, "We'll get you back up to speed in no time." Stew looked around the room and saw the cheeseburgers, "Cook been taking care of you?"

"Oh yeah," Haven shook his head, "They have been. I had some steak and the best mashed potatoes. I even had some apple pie. All the things I've missed."

Stew looked over and studied Haven. He put his hand on Haven's shoulder, "Man, I missed you. Good to see you. Glad you held on and kept yourself alive."

Haven nodded as his eyes squinted slightly. It was as if in one split second, all the memories from the past several years rushed through his mind. The lights in his face. The torture the guerillas loved to inflict. Sleeping on a concrete floor and the sudden bangs that would jar him awake.

Stew had no idea what was going through Haven's mind, but he could imagine it wasn't anything good, "Hey Haven, I've got something for you. I'll be right back."

Haven nodded as Stew left the room. His mind was still back there in the cell, but he was slowly pulling himself out of it. He loved Stew's surprise when The Colonel returned with a cooler full of cold beers. Suddenly, Haven snapped out of it. He knew he was home when he had a cold beer in his hand.

That first drink went down so smooth. In all the time Haven spent thinking about things in his lonely cell, the taste of a cold beer never crossed his mind. But that first drink sure made him miss it. He took a drink, looked at the bottle, and then took another long drink. His first beer was gone in no time.

Stew looked on with a smile on his face, "I can imagine." He popped open another one and handed it to Haven. Then, he repeated himself, "I can only imagine."

They sat for hours talking about things. Both of them did their best to stay off the topic of what life was like in a POW camp. When they found their conversation slipping into that, they changed it quickly. They knew Haven was going to have to work through those thoughts and memories in some sort of therapy or whatever way was more effective for him but now was not the time.

"Oh hey," Stew piped up to change the subject, "I've got something else for you."

"What's that," Haven asked.

"Well, when the Marine Corps processes you and gets all the paperwork straight, I think I've got an opportunity that you'll like," Stew looked at Haven with a nod.

"You don't think retirement would suit me," Haven asked with a smile.

"See, here's the thing," Stew answered, "It's not hard work at all. You don't even work every day. It's consulting for the military, but it's not a 9 to 5 in a suit and tie. I think you'll like it and the pay is very good."

Haven took another drink of his beer and then nodded hard. He was seriously thinking about it. From a cold cell to a job opportunity, all Haven could do was shake his head in disbelief how fast life could change!

§

Skip came down the steps in the middle of the night. He had woken up in an empty bed and normally, that would be odd. But things had changed since he had found out that Haven Kayd was still alive.

Monica was on the couch looking out the window into the moonlight. She had napkins in her hands and her nose was running, sure signs she had been crying. She loved the idea that Haven was still alive. She loved that her daughter still had a father. But she had a problem.

When she was told her husband had died on a mission, all life had stopped for her. She had a daughter to raise on her own and nothing else mattered. She had little time to mourn because a little girl running around the house was a full-time job. But she mourned at night while her daughter slept peacefully. Before long, the need to mourn faded and she knew she needed to get on with life.

She met Skip at her daughter's school. Two single parents taking their kids to a fair that the school had put together. They bumped into each other at the Ring Toss, and then Skip invited her to the Shooting Range where he won her a rubber snake. He tried to work his way up to the Teddy Bear, but the snake was as far as he got.

They married nearly two years later, and Skip was the man Lara now knew as Dad. "Dad" was but a concept to her, the man of the house. That's all she knew about it since her real father had been taken away from her at such an early age.

Skip sat down on the couch with Monica. He sat silently and looked out the window himself. The reality of Haven Kayd being alive wasn't just a heavy matter on Monica's shoulders. It was weighing on him as well.

Monica looked at Skip and studied his eyes, "I'm sorry. I'm just a mess."

Skip tilted his head, "No need to be sorry, honey. You had no idea. How could you?"

Monica's eyes froze on Skip's. She didn't know what to say because her mind was racing a million miles a minute, and then tears dripped from her eyes, "This is so unfair to you."

Skip shook his head, "No. This is unfair to you. I can't imagine what you're going through. Whatever it is, we'll deal with it."

"What do you mean," Monica asked.

Skip put his head down and then looked back up at her with a serious look on his face, "I know how hard this has to be on you. You were married to him. You loved him. You didn't know…"

Monica put her hand on his hand and stopped him, "I'm married to you now. I'm married to you. Don't think that. I'm not thinking that. It's going to be hard to have that conversation with him and I want to be there for him if he needs me. But I think it's going to be best to just let him go and let him get on with putting the pieces of his life back together. I just want him and Lara to have something. You know?"

"I do," Skip nodded, and then he smiled while a quick sigh of relief escaped his lips.

"Oh honey," Monica reached up and touched his face, "Were you worried about that? You don't have to worry about that. You're my husband now. Life gave Haven and me a really bad deal. But that's all it was and you're my husband now. Okay?"

Skip studied Monica with a smile and a tear escaped his eye, "Okay."

"Okay?"

"Okay," Skip pulled Monica toward him and kissed her passionately as if he had just watched his life flash before his eyes and he had survived.

§

In a white dress and her long hair braided behind her back, Lara stood patiently waiting. She was excited but she was fighting her nervous energy while trying to stand as still as possible. With her feet tapping and hands not knowing what to do with themselves, her restlessness couldn't be entirely beat. But she was doing the best she could.

Monica looked equally restless in her floral pattern dress and cork heels. Her fingers were nicely manicured, but she was picking so much at it, they were about to lose their perfect sheen.

Skip was standing behind the girls. He was the least invested in Haven's return and looked the most nervous. He wore a suit and tie to the occasion. He had come into the marriage knowing he had big shoes to fill. But now that Haven was alive, it felt to Skip like the shoes just got a lot bigger. He was a hero being celebrated for surviving years in a POW camp that was abandoned one day for some unknown reason and Haven was left to die alone. There were so many unanswered questions, but Skip could see in Lara's eyes that he would never be able to hold a candle to her real father.

The meeting was scheduled to take place at the Welcome Center at MCAS Cherry Point in North Carolina where Haven would finish being processed out of the Marine Corps. As Monica and Lara patiently waited at the glass doors, Haven's car finally arrived. He was being driven to the Welcome Center and given VIP treatment. The entire day had been planned for him to spend with his family.

A Corporal stepped out of the driver's seat and opened the back door. Lara could feel butterflies rise in her throat. The anticipation was killing her. But the man who stepped out of the back seat was not her father. He was not the man she remembered.

A look of shock registered on Monica's face. She couldn't believe the shape Haven was in. He didn't look well at all. It had been a few weeks from the time he had been saved and that was not enough time to get him completely back to health. Monica had been briefed on his condition, but she could never have imagined that it was that bad.

The Deeper Dark

Lara shook her head as she watched her father walk up to the doors and then as they opened, he walked through. The look on his face was priceless. He lit up when he saw Monica and Lara standing together. His face twisted as he tried to hold back tears.

Lara looked at her mother confused, but Monica nodded subtly. The young lady's eyes went to the man standing at the door and then back to her mother. So, Monica whispered, "Honey, go say hi to your father."

Haven understood. Lara was four years old the last time she saw him. He could see she was struggling to remember him, so he walked over and knelt in front of her. He used to do that when she was small and he wanted to have a heart to heart with her, but she wasn't so small anymore.

To his surprise, Lara tilted her head and smiled. She got on her knees and looked him in his eyes. With a long look and a soft heart, she could start to see him. She was starting to remember the man who was hidden in there somewhere.

Her eyes filled with tears as her memory began to reconcile with the very limited details the Marines had given her about her father's life in a POW camp. Her heart sunk as she felt pity for the man and she hurt for him as her imagination wandered about what he had been through. She could see it in his face that those years had been tough on him and she couldn't help herself but to reach out to the man in front of her. His heart swelled as he hugged her back and pulled her to him. Her arms felt so good around him, the warmest and most tender hug he had ever felt.

Monica put her hands to her mouth as a wave of emotion came over her. Haven looked up at her while still holding his daughter tight. Then, he kissed her on the forehead and stood up to meet his wife.

She choked on her tears when she tried to say, "Hello." He put his arms around her and held her like she was the only person on the face of the earth. When Lara joined and put her arms around them both, Haven felt his life come back together. He could get through anything as long as he had his two girls, the two girls that were in his arms.

The hug lasted a moment and then Haven took a step back, "I know. I know I look like the Crypt Keeper, but I won't for long. I just need a few more steak and potatoes. I'll get back to what I was like in no time."

"No. No, honey," Monica interrupted, "You don't look like...that. It's just...you need...time. It will take a little time. That's all."

Haven's heart was content. Her words were warm and healing. As he studied her face, he noticed the man standing behind her. He noticed his hand on Monica's shoulders and then, he noticed his ring. He looked down and noticed her ring. Immediately, there was a hole in his chest where a heart used to be. He covered it with his hand as he looked back up at the man standing behind his wife.

Monica nodded, "Haven, this is Skip."

Skip extended his hand out and Haven shook it. His lip started to tremble, but Haven tried to hold back all other emotion, "Hi, Skip."

"Hi, Haven," Skip's voice beamed into Haven's ears.

Haven swallowed hard as if his mouth suddenly went dry. His face was showing deep, hurt emotion and the silence was awkward. Too awkward for Monica to stand, "I'm sorry, Haven. They told me...They told me...I raised our daughter for years by myself and then, I met Skip." Monica stopped herself. She knew it wasn't making Haven feel any better about the situation. His face was registering more hurt with every word she said.

He looked over at his daughter. At a moment when he felt like he had just lost everything that ever mattered to him, looking at his daughter reminded him that he still had something left. And that little girl of his was so special, she was enough. She was all he needed in a world that felt like it had completely abandoned him.

That's when he heard his daughter say, "Dad is a good man. You'd like him...Dad." Lara's face went red. She suddenly realized what she had just done, "I'm sorry. Um..."

Like a gut punch, Haven felt the weight of what it was like to be left behind and replaced by someone else. Of course, Lara didn't mean to hurt her father. It was a Freudian Slip, but one like a sharp stake to the heart.

He looked up at Skip who winced when he saw the hurt in Haven's eyes. Then, he looked back at Lara as he reached out to stroke her hair, "It's okay, honey. There are a lot of things we've all gone through. It's going to take a little time to get used to them all. I'm glad he's a good man."

"But, you're my dad," Lara confirmed. Skip nodded knowingly. Lara was all Haven had left. Skip knew he was going to have to give that its own space.

Monica gave it a pause and then interrupted the heavy moment, "Haven, we're going to go. When you get settled, let us know where you are and we can make any kind of arrangements you need."

Her words dropped heavily on his ears. What he thought was going to be a happy family reunion turned into the most heartbreaking moment of his life. Instead of going home with his family, his family was going home without him. His beautiful wife was with someone else and his daughter called him Dad. Throughout all the briefings Haven had been through, nothing prepared him for that.

They said their final goodbyes. He hugged his daughter tight once more and then, he watched them all walk away. He held his hands out in front of him and looked at them long and hard. They were empty. In a very real sense, he had actually been left empty-handed.

Chapter III

"My rumors have a better life than I do."

Months had passed and Haven was feeling more of himself day by day, but every day was another reminder that the world had sort of gone on without him. He had no deranged illusions that the world would stop if he wasn't in it. It's just a weird feeling to come back to civilization feeling like you fell asleep in the 50s and woke up in a world more like in *The Jetsons*.

With the internet in every house and a cellphone in everyone's hands, life was a lot different than what he remembered. It wasn't as if he didn't know what they were. These new gadgets just weren't as popular back in the day before he went missing and was counted out as one of the dead.

When Haven saw how he could conduct a meeting on his smartphone, the world suddenly became full of even greater possibilities. He didn't let the technology stump him. Just the opposite. He was all for learning how it worked. The whole world was connected wirelessly with devices all over the place and every single soul on the face of the earth was recording videos of everything that was happening to keep the rest of the world up to date all the time. It was as if technology had taken quantum leaps while he was in time out in Afghanistan.

He had settled into his new job quite nicely. When Stew had promised him it wouldn't be suit and tie, it turned out to be better than that. It was the most laid-back job Haven ever had. He was a military consultant but that only meant he had an office in D.C. that collected dust most of the time.

He mainly attended video meetings from the comfort of his apartment, a place he had found near his daughter in Clearwater, Florida. Most of the time, he didn't even wear pants. He could easily be on a video chat in the middle of the day and he found no need to dress for the occasion.

Sometimes, the military would fly him to various bases where he would walk around in a polo shirt and blue jeans while watching soldiers train in sweat and tears. Those were days he did not miss. He watched young soldiers full of promise and shook his head. He wouldn't wish what he had gone through on anybody and he hoped these troops would never even see anything like it.

That was the gist of his job and it paid very well, but it gave him a good bit of downtime. Instead of twiddling his thumbs while he sat for hours in a lonely apartment, he decided to dominate this new world of technology. What gave him the idea was when he created his profile on social media. After telling the world who he was and adding a photo, his profile blew up with followers. They already knew who he was and before he knew it, his profile had gone viral.

At first, he didn't know what to post. It was hard to imagine anything anyone would want to hear about how his day went, what he had to eat, what he thought, or what he planned to do for the rest of the day. His feed was full of people telling their life stories and most of the posts were literally down to the minute detail by detail as if they had replaced actual living with their life on Facebook.

It was when Haven started posting about his military experiences that his posts blew up with thousands of likes. He figured that must be a good thing. His followers ate it up. Even when he talked about simple training exercises or jokes he shared with Marines when he served, his posts were very popular. That's what gave him the idea to create a website. Sharing stories was fun. Why not share them from his site?

He soon found out that wasn't much of a task. The hardest part about it was coming up with a domain. When he did his research, he found a website package that was easy to install, and within five minutes he was up and running. It was a little depressing to him. He thought it would be some major job that turned out to be the easiest task in the world. He had set aside his whole day to figure out how to build a website and he wasn't even finished his first drink before he was staring at it, up and running on the web for the whole world to see.

And that's how his hunger for the internet grew. Working with WordPress at an amateur level allowed him to learn some code when he got into the more advanced ways of manipulating his website. Once he started writing code, he became addicted. He started Googling everything and watching Youtube videos. The more he learned, the more he wanted to learn.

Before long, he found himself learning about the dark web. It was far from a few keystrokes away. He found it intriguing how to access networks that weren't available on the Clearnet and some of the things he found there were very disturbing. Next to sex films, people loved watching snuff films of actual victims dying. Another part of the dark web Haven found disturbing was how much stolen military equipment was for sale. But when he learned that a person could literally buy a baby, it shook his soul. He almost got out of the dark web and never went back.

Putting more pieces of the puzzle back together, Haven started trying to have a social life. But he had forgotten how to do that a long time ago. When he started dating Monica all those years ago, his bar life came to a screeching halt and that was the last time he needed to get out and meet people. His friends were military friends and his life was his wife.

Going out now was awkward. He was older than everybody in the clubs. He tried sitting at a bar and talking, but that got old quick. He hated when someone would ask his name and then everyone would make a fuss over him. They would ask him all kinds of questions and there was no filter. Drunk people excited to have a hero in their presence have no consideration for the questions they ask. From what life was like in the POW camp to what was he doing over there in the first place, it all made him cringe and he started going to bars less and less.

But his social life was about to change the day he got an extraordinary phone call. A producer was interested in turning his story into a movie. For some reason, that seemed a lot different than a whole bunch of drunks yelling random questions at him in the middle of a bar. Telling his story to Hollywood suddenly sounded very interesting. It also came with a nice paycheck, which was another bonus.

The Deeper Dark

That's how he met Detective Carlos Jimenez. They were both consultants on the film. The detective was a regular at consulting on films because he knew investigative work and he was also prior military. He had served in the Army for eight years and he was pretty much the big man on the block when it came to advising directors and actors throughout the making of a movie.

That was until Haven walked on the set for the first time. Carlos couldn't help himself from being a little starstruck. After all, he had gone in the Army a year after Captain Kayd was captured in Afghanistan. Haven had been fighting battles for years before Carlos was even old enough to sign. There was not only the huge difference of military experience between them, but there was also the issue of seniority and of course the fact that this particular film was about the man everyone had started calling "The Captain." Obviously, Carlos knew of him and he wanted to know even more. But he was determined not to come across like a screaming elementary school kid excited about seeing a rock star.

"Haven, what do you think," yelled Mitch Lasner, the director of *Left for Dead*.

Haven was working with an actor who looked just like him when he heard Mitch call his name. He looked over to see that they were finished with the cell. Haven wasn't really looking forward to this inspection. Instead of a flashback, this was an actual life-size replica of the place he had called home for years until his escape.

As Haven approached, he noticed two cells. One was just three concrete walls and the other was two concrete walls with the door. Haven could feel an uneasiness rise within him. Even though there were no ceilings and only three walls to each cell, they gave him the feeling of being back in there.

"You okay," Carlos's voice broke through the tension.

Haven's eyes had been locked on the door for the longest time. Mitch kept looking back and forth between it and Haven, trying to figure out what he was looking at so intensely. When Carlos spoke, it was a welcome interruption.

"Oh hey, detective," Mitch greeted.

Carlos nodded at Mitch and then looked at Haven, "It's an exact replica, isn't it?"

Haven looked over at Carlos, "It is. I was there again for a minute."

"Whoa! I'm sorry," Mitch genuinely apologized.

"Don't be," Haven consoled, "It's good. They'll definitely get the story. But there's one thing."

"What's that," Mitch asked.

Haven walked up to the door and pointed at the concrete, "There was a crack about here. That's how I was able to work the bolt free. I worked it with my fingers until they bled just to get enough give and break away even the smallest piece of concrete. As long as the pieces kept falling, I kept going."

Carlos shook his head, "Wow!" He looked at the door as he imagined what that would be like, "The script doesn't tell half the story, does it?"

"Well, it's as close as Bill wanted it to get to the real thing at first," Mitch answered, "I can do rewrites based on the notes we got from Haven. I've been able to talk Bill into making it as real as possible."

"Are you sure you want to do that," Carlos asked.

"No. No," Haven interrupted, "Real is best. Days spent in here going in and out of sleep. Working every single waking minute to get out while hunger ate up my insides and my head pounded constantly. Those are the things you can't make the audience feel. But you can still tell the story."

"And you don't think that would be too much for certain people in the audience," Carlos asked.

"Well, you give people a warning," Haven looked Carlos dead in the eyes, "But you can't hold their hand."

Carlos nodded, "No one held yours, did they?"

Haven laughed, "No, they didn't. No, they did not."

That's when it dawned on Mitch, "Oh hey Haven, this is Detective Carlos Jimenez. He's an active detective, but we bring him on films to help us get the details right." Then, Mitch looked at Carlos, "Detective, this is Haven. Captain Haven Kayd of the United States Marine Corps."

"Oh, I know who he is, Mitch," Carlos responded, and then turned to Haven, "It's a pleasure to meet you."

"Likewise, Detective," Haven said as he held out his hand.

"Please, call me Carlos."

"Okay, Carlos it is then," Haven beamed as the two shook hands.

Carlos and Haven felt right at home kicking back in beach chairs while putting down some beers in the studio parking lot at Haven's trailer. Haven kicked off his shoes and enjoyed the feel of his bare feet against the warm pavement under the hot Hollywood sun. Of course, it was cooling off for the evening even though people were still taking tours of the studios and trollies kept riding by every so often with passengers Haven hilariously cheered every time they passed.

As Haven reached in the cooler for a few more beers, Carlos looked around at the trailer, "Must be nice to get a trailer."

Haven looked at him with a half-cocked grin, "You don't have one?"

Carlos shook his head and laughed, "I'm just kidding. I live here. I live just outside of Los Angeles."

"Oh," Haven saluted him with his beer, "This is a good gig for you then?"

"It's a great one. I wouldn't be able to afford my home if it weren't for picking up consulting gigs like this every once in a while," Carlos answered. He took a drink and then he thought, "Speaking of which, I should have you over to the house for a BBQ or something. My son is a fan of yours. It would make me a real somebody in his eyes if I were to bring you home with me one day."

"Hey, I'm always up for a BBQ," Haven nodded. He studied his beer and then a thought occurred to him, "So, you're still a detective?"

"Yeah, I still do the job. Getting ready to retire soon, though," Carlos answered, "I lucked out. I'm actually working a case right now, but I set my schedule to come here when they put together the production board and it's all very flexible."

"So, you're like *CSI* and everything," Haven grinned.

"Uh, more like *Law and Order*," Carlos corrected.

"Ah, the nitty-gritty nuts and bolts of it," Haven understood.

"Yeah, that *CSI* is too much styling and profiling for me," Carlos responded.

Carlos had a few more beers and then ordered a Lyft. It was a good time he just couldn't pass up, but he knew he was in no shape to drive home. That left Haven to himself in his trailer. It was nice. He had no complaints, but there was too much day left for him. He took a walk to grab a coffee and see what else he could get into, but that walk turned into a restless mess. Trying to burn some time, but it only took ten minutes to get to the coffee shop. Walking around and seeing what else he could get into only took him another twenty minutes.

The evening just seemed to drag into the night, so he resigned himself back to his trailer with the idea that he would write an article for his site. At least, he had something interesting to say. Who wouldn't want to know what life was like on set when the movie was his own story? His fans loved those articles and the more they went viral, the more followers he gained.

After publishing his article with pictures he had taken that day, he thought he'd check his emails real quick and then watch some TV in bed until he fell asleep. They weren't the greatest evening plans, but life didn't have to go a hundred miles per hour all the time.

That's when a particularly interesting email caught his eye. When he looked at who it was from, Casper Seuss was about as fake of a name as it gets. A Ghost Storyteller, the easiest mystery to crack. Plus, there was absolutely no other information associated with it. That was one red flag.

The subject line read, "Just For You Captain." That meant he didn't know this person personally, but the individual knew him. He quickly ran the email through malware detection software he had downloaded from the dark web, but he knew enough to reverse engineer anything he downloaded from shady servers. Haven was a quick study and he had caught on quick to the game.

When the email came up clean, he decided to open it and see what it was about. It was a simple message with a link, "The production of your cute little film might come to an abrupt halt. Some higher-ups are concerned the movie might get too real."

Haven rubbed his chin as he digested those words. When he looked at the link, he could tell it was from a deep site Google had no idea existed. Haven wasn't ready to click on it yet. He wasn't hesitant because it might take him to a site full of viruses that would raise havoc on his laptop. He had a gut feeling that wouldn't be the case. The sender seemed to be genuinely trying to tell him something. What Haven did have hesitations about was taking a step onto a site and leaving footprints. He didn't know everything yet, but he had reservations about walking around too much in the deep web where his identity could be found out and tracked for hundreds of reasons, neither of which were any good.

Chapter IV

"If you thought things were going to go smooth, you haven't been paying attention your whole life."

Haven felt like he had just been put through the third degree, but Danny was a good boy. He meant well. He was just so interested in everything Haven had to say and it seemed like every story Haven told him prompted a whole slew of new questions.

When Carlos had said something about a BBQ, Haven took him seriously. He wasn't about to let the detective get away with an empty promise. In fact, he made a thing out of it. He had Lara flown out to California to spend part of the summer in a vacation condo for a week. Then, they would return to Florida together.

While getting in some much-needed quality father and daughter time, Haven was determined to fit a nice BBQ into their plans. Carlos' wife Jennifer threw it down in the kitchen and made Red Skin Potato Salad as well as an interesting Cheese and Guacamole Dip for chips. She even made some dessert.

But Carlos was king of the grill with his apron and professional grill tool kit. He was grilling chicken and ribs that he had marinated all night. Grilling wasn't just a fun way to cook food, but it was practically a religion to him. It had to be done right and his apron said it best, "No meat should be grilled before its time."

It didn't take long for Carlos and Haven to notice that Danny's heart was doing flips over Lara. They were about the same age and Danny was thinking of anything in the world to talk to her about. He asked her about her school and what she liked to do on weekends. Lara was a little shy at first, but she started to open up. And then unknowingly, Carlos blocked his own son's game when he dropped the big bomb in the middle of the conversation.

"You know, I'm sorry about the movie," Carlos said as he flipped the chicken on the grill. He shrugged his shoulders and continued, "It happens once in a while. I've seen movies canceled before there was budgeting, but I have also seen some canceled after they started filming too."

"That is a bad deal, dad," Lara said as her attention went from Danny to her father, "I thought that was cool they were making a movie about you."

"Yeah, Mr. Kayd," Danny added, "I wanted to see it."

"I don't think I could have watched it," Lara looked at Danny, "It was going to be pretty real by what I heard."

Danny nodded, "Oh yeah, that would be rough. I mean, for you. I get that." Lara's eyes locked on his and her face softened slightly.

Haven noticed and it made him grin that sparks might be flying at such a young age. That's when he decided to add a small wrinkle to the story, "Actually, I had a hint it was coming."

"You did," Carlos and Jennifer both asked in unison.

"Carlos had no idea," Jennifer added.

As Carlos and Jennifer stared at Haven patiently waiting to hear how he knew, the question lingered for a moment before Haven let the name "Casper Seuss" roll from his lips with a steady tone.

"Who," Carlos asked.

"That's all I know about him," Haven tilted his head, "He wrote me an email letting me know this might happen."

"And you don't know who he is or anything more about it," Carlos asked.

Haven nodded, "There was a link in the email, but I haven't clicked it yet."

"Why not," Carlos asked.

Haven shook his head and then looked at Carlos with the most intense look, "It's one of those links to a site Google knows nothing about. I've been hesitant about leaving any footprints in that part of the internet."

"Are you talking about the deep web," Danny asked.

"Yeah," Haven answered, "It's not the place to play around."

Danny whispered in Lara's direction, "Your dad is so cool. This is like real-life spy stuff."

Lara smiled at Danny and then looked at her father, "I know, right?"

"Well, what did the email say," Jennifer asked.

"Just that higher-ups thought the movie was going to be too real," Haven answered.

"I knew it," Carlos said as he shook his head and waved his spatula in the air, "Get some old vets in the theater or anyone suffering from PTSD and that movie had the potential to cause some real problems. I wanted to tell the true story too. But some people just can't handle it."

Haven rubbed his chin as he considered Carlos' words, "I'm not sure that's what they meant."

"What do you mean," Carlos asked.

"Well, Mitch said he could do rewrites. If higher-ups were pressuring him not to make it too real, I think he would have rewritten those parts. I don't think that's what Casper Seuss was talking about," Haven answered.

"I get the Casper part. He's a ghost," Danny said trying to show off his IQ, "But Seuss? I don't get that."

"Have you ever read a Dr. Seuss book," Haven asked.

"Oh," Danny's eyes lit up with surprise, "He's uh...a uh..."

"I got it," Lara chimed in, "He tells stories."

Haven snapped his fingers and pointed at Lara, "And the prize goes to..."

"That's so cool," Danny commented.

"What'd I win dad," Lara joked.

"You have won an all-expenses-paid trip to California to spend time with your dad," Haven answered.

"I'm already doing that," Lara joked, "I want something else. I feel ripped off."

As the laughter faded, Carlos looked over at Haven, "What do you think he meant by real then?"

Haven looked off into the distance as his wheels were turning, "I think there's more to the story than what I was telling. These so-called higher-ups might be afraid that those details might find their way into the movie."

"Like, what kind of details," Carlos asked.

"That's the part I don't know," Haven answered, "If I let my imagination run wild, I'd say it might have something to do with why the compound was abandoned and I was the only one left behind."

"You think we had something to do with that," Carlos asked.

"I wouldn't imagine," Haven answered, "But it is something I'd like to find out."

"Well, you can begin by following that link," Carlos urged.

"I'd like to know more about the guy who sent me the email first," Haven said, "I'd feel better looking into the link if I knew who sent it to me."

"Well, you can track the header information and get an ISP that can lead you to an identity if you know what you're doing with that sort of thing," Danny mentioned nonchalantly.

Haven's head snapped around at Danny, "You know something about it?"

"I play around," Danny looked at Lara and saw the intrigue in her expression.

"Yeah, kids his age are all over that stuff. It's also a part of detective work," Carlos chimed in, "We have an IT guy who does all that. But working with him, it tends to rub off."

"Header information," Haven nodded as his eyes rolled up to the right, "I'll look into that."

"Anything I can do to help," Danny stated with confidence.

Carlos smiled, "Who's ready for chicken?"

"I know I am," Haven's face lit up. He looked at his daughter and did a funny gesture with his eyebrows. Watching her laugh was the light of his soul.

§

Lara and Haven spent a great week together. They took in Disneyland and the Walk of Fame. They did some shopping and some fine dining. Even though Lara loved her father's attempts to take her out to nice meals, she was fine with cheeseburgers in hole-in-the-wall joints. In fact, she preferred them, and when Haven finally realized that he learned yet another thing he had in common with his daughter.

He wasn't going to stop trying though. He figured out what he could do to blow her mind. Not as if he needed to do anything special to impress her, being her father was enough for her. But having missed out on years of her life, Haven subconsciously was trying to play catch up and another thing he wasn't fully aware of was that he was competing against Skip. The subconscious can be a tricky thing full of illusions and misinformation. But when she slipped and called Skip "Dad" in front of him, it embedded itself into Haven's psyche so deeply that even he wasn't aware of how deep that scar went.

On their day to leave, Haven got them a limo to the airport. But instead of getting dropped off at the airline entrances, the car entered a private gate and drove up to a small plane sitting on the tarmac. Haven had made plans to fly his daughter home himself and he made her the copilot. Let Skip try to beat that!

§

When Haven finally got home and settled in, he poured himself a drink and decided he'd dig right into the mysterious email from Casper Seuss. His strategy was very logical. He would Google to see if the software he needed existed and if it did, he would get it from servers on the dark web. Of course, he would reverse engineer it to remove any malware, and then he'd be up and running.

The first software he Googled was to track the header of an email. What he found was how unbelievably easy it was to get an IP address from the header and then simply Google that for information. That's where he found a big loophole mess. The sender knew what he was doing and for some reason, Haven started to feel less and less intimidated. It was as if the more Casper did to hide his identity, the more he came across as a credible source. It might seem like backward logic. But the more a person spends on the dark web, the more backward logic starts to make sense.

Haven wasn't giving up though. He downloaded some interesting header software anyway and reverse engineered it until he felt safe enough to use. The long string of IP information led him to an address in D.C. When he looked into it further, it was from a government building. Immediately, Haven felt his heart drop as his face went numb.

Someone within the government had informed him that his movie was going to be canceled because "higher-ups thought it was going to get too real." That's when Haven's fears were confirmed. There were details to his own story that even he didn't know. He wasn't sure he wanted to know, but there was that side of him that wouldn't let it go.

That's when he received a notification about a new email. It was from Casper. He hesitated to open it up, but he decided to trust his gut and go for it.

Casper: Captain, I see you've done your homework and found out that I am in the government. Cease and desist from trying to find out further about me. Your focus should be on the link I sent you. It has the information you're looking for. You can trust the link even though I'm quite sure you won't.

Haven grabbed his drink and sat back on his couch. He wanted more than ever to click on the link and now, he felt better about doing it. It was that backward logic at work again, but the tone of the email and the words in it made him feel like this was a friend on the inside and not someone with malicious intentions. Haven knew that Casper might have his own agenda and that sat perfectly fine with him. Whatever was motivating Casper was serving Haven's purpose and that made him "a friendly" to a certain extent.

He took a drink and went Googling for more software. Even though it was true Haven considered Casper a friendly, he wasn't about to let his guard down that easy. What he found on the dark web was software that would allow him to explore a link from all angles. Who owned the domain? Was malware attached when the link was accessed? What would he see if he clicked the link?

Who owned the domain was a little confusing. It was on a private server, but there was government-grade protection. That sent up a red flag that the site might contain confidential information from the government. No malware was attached obviously, and the site was stripped of any excessive design. It was simply full of information and something on it pertained to Haven.

He investigated it thoroughly and then when he was sure it was safe, he finally clicked the link. That's when his world started to turn upside down. It was like a thread on a sweater that you hesitate to pull because everything will begin to unravel. Haven had no idea what he had just stepped into, but he was about to find out the truth about everything and the real story wasn't going to make him happy at all.

Chapter V

"Some people are so accident-prone, I don't know how they're going to make it through life without dying."

When Haven clicked the link, it took him to a forum where a lot of information was being shared. But the link wasn't just to the forum, it went straight to a specific topic:

"Captain Kayd False Sortie"

Haven studied the headline for a moment. He couldn't believe he was being discussed in deep dark places of the net that few people even knew existed. They talked about him like he was a fixed name in history as if they not only knew of him but they knew more about him than he knew about himself. Diving into the comments, that's where he found some disturbing information.

Post: Leaked documents reveal the Captain's mission wasn't necessary. His recording equipment wasn't even on.

The Dean: It figures. Most of the stuff we do around the world isn't necessary.

The Missing Man: Can you imagine? He was a POW for years and he had no business even flying that mission.

Big D: What I'd like to know is why?

"I'd like to know that too, Big D," Haven thought as he read through more comments before returning to the original post. There was a link in the post that took him to a document. It was the transcripts of text messages that were brief in nature, but they made their point.

Redacted Number: No recording.

Redacted Number: It's an intel mission.

Redacted Number: We just need the plane in the area at that time.

Redacted Number: Why not record anyway? Might as well get footage?

Redacted Number: Do not record! NO RECORDING!

Redacted Number: You got it.

"Why would they turn off the recording equipment? Why did they just want me in the area," Haven had many questions. But he could only ask himself. He wasn't about to join the conversation and let the forum members know he was there. He did go back and start reading comments again. Down, down, down he scrolled until he found some comments that shed light on the subject.

Dude Red: I think those redacted numbers were uncovered and they aren't military. They're in Washington Offices.

Master Qi: Not pentagon?

Dude Red: Definitely not pentagon.

Master Qi: Who gives orders to the military other than the military?

Try Me: Well uh, Congress.

Master Qi: Well sure. They declare war and the president is the CIC. But why would some Washington Office be giving the command to cut off recording equipment?

Try Me: Not only that but why is someone in Washington even interested in micromanaging a mission to that detail?

All Haven could do was nod his head. What these guys were talking about was making perfect sense. They were asking the right questions. Haven was restless. He was beside himself. He thought of making a few phone calls and ruffling a few feathers and then he thought of something much better. He decided to take the story public.

Anyone in their right mind would have advised him against it, but no one in their right mind was around to do that. It certainly is one danger of the internet. Give a man the ability to broadcast information at any time, then just add alcohol. How many posts across the net were born from the hilarious combination of drama and intoxication? Off to writing Haven went and a very angrily worded article was published within the hour.

He sat back and looked at his work. Then, nodded as he took another drink. He felt a little better because he had gotten it all off his chest, but that didn't make a dent in how disgusted he was that the recording equipment was ordered off and why would his mission have absolutely no purpose? His time as a POW was the years he could have been home with his daughter, with his wife, enjoying his life instead of rotting away in a cell! The more he thought about it, the more disgusted he became.

He found himself scrolling through other headlines on the forum. There was a lot there. How these guys got the information they were sharing, he had no idea. This was stuff that could send countries to war, end careers, and send the American people into hysteria.

At first, he just scrolled headlines. He popped into some topics and read the comments, then backed out when it felt like his brain had melted and was oozing out of his ears. He simply could not believe what he was finding. Of course, it wasn't all about him. In fact, only a small percentage of it was. It was heavy stuff nonetheless and it was hard to believe any of it was true.

Haven was moving very slow when he woke up the next morning. He stumbled to the kitchen to make some coffee. He rooted around in cabinets that had no business have anything to do with coffee in them. When he finally got it together and turned the coffee maker on, he stood at the sink and listened to the perking sound of some strong brew coming to life.

When he finally made a cup, he poured himself onto the couch and rested for a moment with his hand on his head. Drinking had never been a problem for him. But drinking at his age was starting to have those nasty morning side effects.

After taking a few drinks of coffee, he reached for his laptop and fired it up. When he logged onto his computer, that's when he realized what he had done. His article had gone viral and there were thousands of comments on his site. Most of them were sympathetic. Some of them were anti-war debris. It didn't matter to him what the comments were, his article had gained some traffic and even though it made him cringe for a second when he remembered writing it, he was proud of his work and he wasn't about to back down from it.

§

About a thousand miles away in a little town known as Washington, D.C., the reception of Haven's article wasn't quite the same. It was definitely in the many whispers that were circling the capital. If you can imagine the picture, some politicians were scratching their heads while others were smirking. That's one special relationship they have in the great divide that exists in The District. When one side is involved in a scandal, the other side gets to smirk and use it to their advantage any way they can.

But on top of the hill, there was a lady who seemed particularly interested in the article. She sat down on a couch in the East Wing and scrolled through the article on her tablet as she whispered to herself, "Where is he getting his information? They turned the recording equipment off. They sent a plane out for no reason at all. And he was the pilot of that plane. Captain Haven Kayd. I never even knew you existed, but I do now."

Sarah Fulton was a beautiful lady with straight blond hair who had aged well. She was in her fifties and she was just like a fine wine. She used to be a model, which is how she helped her husband's shoe business expand. Then, she took a turn as a Senator before becoming the First Lady.

Sarah was in the middle of typing a text message when her assistant popped in the office, "Your meeting with the Homeless Single Mothers is ready. They're already here, ma'am."

Sarah looked up with a distant look in her eyes. She stared at her assistant for a moment and then, as if coming back to earth, "I'll be right there."

"Yes ma'am. I'll let them know."

"Good," Sarah nodded. As the assistant left the office, the First Lady went back to her text. She read it first and then typed some more before pushing send. She studied her phone for a moment and then stared out into space as if in deep thought about something.

Back in Florida, Haven was already beyond his controversial article. He was looking through the underground forum for more information about his mission. He didn't know what was going to turn up, but he had a lot of questions. An answer to any one of them would have sufficed.

He was disappointed that he couldn't find any other topics at all on the subject. But he knew the forum wasn't all about him. The fact was, he was the least interesting subject on it. The POTUS was the hottest topic of course from how he was handling the conflict in Botswana to how his nose seemed to be getting bigger while in office. Most of the topics throughout the forum though were of scandals all over the place involving such people as CEOs of pharmaceutical companies, directors of charities, celebrities in Hollywood, and even the royalty of monarchies throughout the world.

Haven did a thorough search through the forum and after reading the subjects of post after post, he knew it was no wonder they weren't talking about him much. So, he decided he was going to have to do some digging of his own. The first thing he was going to have to do though was learn how. Of course, hacking was a raw skill that took knowing about how the internet was constructed and how to bypass securities. Most sites were easy to access, but government sites were very difficult.

Plus, he was playing catchup in a world where ten-year-olds were hacking Facebook. He didn't feel like he was in a race though. He was just trying to learn as much as he could so that he could pull more at the thread and see what other secrets came out. Not surprised at all, he found software that would help him hack sites. That made the job a lot easier, but he still had to know what he was doing.

The difference between what he was trying to do and what hackers actually do is what he was looking for. He was looking for very specific information. That was like looking for a needle in a haystack. What hackers mainly do is access private emails and confidential documents to see what they can uncover. They aren't looking for anything specific. In fact, they have no idea what they're going to find.

Searches wouldn't work no matter how specific they were worded. The information he was looking for wouldn't be indexed by any search engine. So, where was he to start? Within the government, there are thousands of locations where documents are stored. It would be nice if they could put everything in one place, but that, to say it nicely, just isn't how it works.

Besides that, if he was going to find the answers to his questions, they weren't simply going to be on straight documents passed around from office to office, classified as confidential, and then archived on a server to collect dust. The information he was looking for would be on obscure documentation that was often overlooked as accessible. That's when people get lazy and drop their guard. They think texts get deleted. They think emails are private between the sender and the receiver. They think memos magically destruct after five seconds. But they couldn't be more wrong.

All information can be accessed. Just ask any hacker who's worth his weight in gold. Deleted files can be resurrected. Any communication transferred over invisible wires can be snatched out of the sky and made public for the whole world to see. This was all working to Haven's benefit. The problem was it felt like it took a thousand years to get through millions of communications about just having lunch. Any normal man would have given up after a day or two, but Haven was no normal man.

After days of searching, he was finally able to find some information about himself. It started with the revelation that Captain Haven Kayd was still alive, a document dated years before his escape. In follow-up emails, there was an order to keep that information confidential. Someone asked if Haven's wife should be informed and the response was negative. Haven could feel the heat rising from his neck. His wife wouldn't have married Skip had she known he was still alive. Why would they keep that from her?

The thing is, Haven wasn't finished yet. There was more to pour through, and the truth was about to get even more heartbreaking for him. It appears that the military was looking into conducting a rescue mission, but it was canceled. The information had come to light that Haven was the only American being held captive in that POW camp. The language in follow-up emails got harder and harder for him to read. One email stated the financial concerns in supporting a mission to save one man from a POW camp with further concerns of how much intel was even reliable. And then, there was the bomb dropped on it all. In the final email Haven looked over, he saw the harsh reality of why the mission was canceled when he read the words, "We can't risk a team and all the support involved just to save one man."

§

In the deeper dark of the internet where hackers have their private conversations, it appears Haven had caught the attention of some very mysterious individuals. These were the guys who liked touching things and they could reach into just about anything they wanted. Even though one of them was only seventeen years old while the other two were much older, it didn't matter. In their world, they were considered equals because they had the power to interrupt the morning news with a brief message, to knock nefarious organizations to their knees by freezing their finances, and in their off-time, just for fun they could shut off the electricity on an entire city.

Octello: It looks like the Captain has been snooping around.

Str8nger: Yeah, he's definitely getting up to speed on what they did to him.

Octello: His article went pretty high.

The Teacher: They read it. The hill never whispered that quietly.

Str8nger: Well, he's done.

The Teacher: I don't know. I don't see any movement.

Octello: They're not acting right away. Doesn't mean they're not coming.

The Teacher: Shall we play a game?

Chapter VI

"Drinking alone isn't as fun when there are people around."

Sarah stared at her husband with tender eyes that pierced right through George's soul. His heart melted when she looked at him that way. She was just as beautiful as the first time he met her, and he could remember that day as if it was yesterday. She had been sent over from the modeling agency to do a photoshoot and a commercial for his bookstore. He was about to grow from one store to two and knew he was going to have to put some money in it to make it fly.

Sarah stole his heart that day and he made her the spokesperson for all the future advertisements. He thought he was slick when he invited her to a business dinner, but she had set her eyes on him too. He didn't have to try as hard as he did. He had no reason to be nervous every time they had a "business meeting" in the name of building his empire. She was just patiently waiting for that moment when he finally turned their business meetings into dates.

They married within a few years while his empire had grown rapidly from two stores to over thirty across the country. That's when she set her eyes on the Senate and he backed her campaign with everything he had. Once she was in office and he got a taste for that kind of power, he set his eyes on his own office. Of course, his ambition was to go straight to the top. It was a little aggressive and some people tried to talk him out of it, but the climate across America was calling for him. They were tired of lawyers and career politicians with their double talk and slick lies. America wanted something new, something fresh. They took one look at George and fell in love.

"Have you read any of his articles," Sarah asked as she held her tablet in George's direction.

"I've been briefed," he answered, "How many articles are we talking about?"

"Well, he's been writing for a while about the military and his experience in the POW camp," she answered, "But the last two articles are different."

"Okay. Those are the ones I've been briefed about," he said.

"So, you know what's in them," she asked.

"What? Why," he returned.

"He's leaking confidential information and who knows how true it is, but it's all going viral and people are talking about it," she answered.

"What kind of leaked information," he asked.

"These briefings you got about these articles are very scary. If this is any indication of how you get briefed, I'd be upset if I was you because they're not telling you anything," she shook her head with her hand on her hip.

He couldn't help but find her actions amusing, "Okay honey, what's in these articles that I need to know about?"

She cocked her head as her stare got even more intense, "He was sent out on an intel mission and he says someone ordered that his recording equipment be shut off. The mission wasn't even necessary."

"That sounds ridiculous," the President shook his head as he looked at himself in the mirror and took off his tie.

"And that's just one article," she continued, "In the follow-up, he writes that we knew he was alive, and we didn't do anything about it. We didn't notify his wife and we didn't even try to save him. In fact, he says that a rescue mission was canceled because and I quote, 'We can't risk a team to get one man.'"

George turned to look at her as he pulled off his dress shirt, "I know it seems harsh, but that's the kind of thinking that goes into those kinds of missions. That would most likely have been an unpopular decision, but one they were forced to make. Besides the fact honey, I wasn't even in office then. I was never briefed about this man. His name never made it up the chain to me. I'm pretty sure I've never talked about this man being held captive in a POW camp. I would remember that."

She nodded subtly as she furled her eyebrow, "Documents that are marked confidential. Emails that were deleted, or at least they should have been. How is he getting this information?"

"That's an issue I inherited," he looked at her with a careless look in his eyes, "We've been dealing with leaks long before I got in office. With hackers out there breaking into the Pentagon and hacking other government offices, it's hardly something new and it's nearly impossible to stop."

"But wouldn't that be considered espionage or something," she asked.

"Yeah, but who's going to get charged with it," he returned.

"Well," she hesitated to say, "He does have this information on his website."

His head turned slowly, and his eyes had the look of confused surprise, "Are you kidding? After all he's been through, that would be committing political suicide. Plus, he's probably not even the one accessing the files. Hackers are most likely leaking this information to him. So, he wouldn't really be guilty of anything. It would be hard to prove anyway."

Sarah climbed into bed and propped herself up with pillows. George wasn't far behind and he could feel her eyes on his every move. When he climbed into bed, he looked over at her to see those beautiful eyes that melted his soul. "Do you really want that," he asked with a softer voice.

She looked him in his eyes for a moment and shook her head slowly with a serious stare, "No. Of course not. He's a hero. He doesn't deserve that."

"Oh. Okay. Good," he nodded and leaned toward her for a goodnight kiss.

§

Haven's second article about the conspiracy he was exposing had gone even more viral than the first. In fact, it had given new traffic to the first article too. Now, there were millions of views and he was gaining followers by the day. His Facebook had blown up and an unofficial Twitter account had been created in his name. He wasn't even running it, but it was keeping thousands, and then tens of thousands of followers updated on new information about The Captain.

It was as if his research and his website had taken on a life of their own. He was knee-deep into finding out more about the story. Were the details he had already uncovered the real details higher-ups were afraid would be revealed or was there more? He wanted to know.

And then one day, he had this odd feeling. He didn't know how to shake it, but it nagged at him all morning. The funny thing about what was nagging at him was a simple case of "out of sight, out of mind." He finally realized what it was. He hadn't been in contact with work for over a week. There had been no phone calls and no emails. His heart dropped a little when he realized what had happened. It was too obvious they had terminated him without letting him know. And the reason was also too obvious, he was making the military and the government look suspect in his case. The American people weren't happy about that and the military didn't like it when the American people turned against it. So, Haven was without a job.

"Well, I guess that just happened," he said to himself, seemingly not fazed at all. He simply popped some Google ads on his site and kept going. Google would pay his rent and with all the traffic he was getting, it would pay him so much more than that. From that moment on, his own story became his full-time job.

§

Baroness Coutts: I was referred to you.

The Mule: I was informed you would be getting a hold of me.

Baroness Coutts: So, you can do what I need?

The Mule: I was given a few details. You'll have to be more specific.

Baroness Coutts: Right. I'm just making sure that you're the guy for the job.

The Mule: Oh, I'm definitely the guy for the job. This just might be the easiest job I've ever done.

Baroness Coutts: I just need you to dig around at first. I need anything that I can use against him.

The Mule: So, don't blow anything up or break anything?

Baroness Coutts: Keep that on the back burner for now. I just need some information.

The Mule: You got it!

§

"Just close your eyes and I am there! It's never too long before we are...together again," Haven closed the pages he had been reading.

It was a beautiful day as they sat on a picnic table underneath a palm tree. Waves from the Gulf of Mexico crashed merely a few feet from them, a truly tranquil place to sit and talk. The sun was still a bit high in the sky, but it was making its way down to bring a nice, cool dusk to their day together.

"That's beautiful, Dad," Lara said with tears in her eyes but a smile on her face, "When did you write that?"

Haven looked at her closely for a moment, "When I was in the cell, I thought of you over and over. I thought of times we were missing. Things we never got to do together and then, they turned into things we were doing. My imagination was so strong, those things became so real to me. It was like I was having a life with you and I hoped if I thought about those things really hard, you would feel them too. That somehow, you would feel a warmth in your heart and get a smile on your face. That way, you would remember me."

Lara dropped her head. Haven watched as he could see tears dropping from her eyes and her little hands were trying to cover them, "Dad, I did." She shook her head and then looked up at him, "We joked around with each other. We swam in a lake and you taught me how to float. You made me a dollhouse."

"I had that one too," Haven smiled as he winced at his daughter, "I had all those." He could feel her pain.

Lara let out a light laugh. She felt a little better like a weight had been lifted, "Those things we did together, all in my head, but they felt so real. They made me feel like I was actually spending time with you...like I still had a father around. It did. It made me feel warm. I did smile."

Haven studied Lara as she hesitated to continue. She looked at him and then she looked away. He could tell the next words were going to be hard for her to say. In fact, he could almost feel what they were.

She softly broke the silence, "Until I looked around and the dollhouse wasn't there. Then, I remembered I was just imagining things. My whole life with my father was a complete imagination. The greatest times of my life were memories of things that never even happened. When they told me...they told me..." She shook her head and cracked a broken smile.

"I know," Haven's broken smile cracked too. He reached out his hand to hers. Once thousands of miles apart, they were together. Once just illusions in each other's imaginations, they could now feel each other. A bond they felt so strongly but were afraid to lose again.

Lara rubbed her thumb across her father's knuckles, "Sometimes, I wonder if this is true. If I'm doing it again."

"I'm here, honey," Haven confirmed.

"Because when they told me you...had died, I stopped," Lara cocked her head as she looked at her father, "I'm sorry. It wasn't easy, but I stopped my head. I stopped my mind from making up all those things. It hurt too much. Imagining a father that was never going to come home, that I was never going to see again. My mind wanted to keep making stuff up, but I made it stop."

"I did too, honey," Haven admitted.

Lara looked at him with surprise at first. Then, she nodded and accepted that it made sense. It made perfect sense.

"I had to stop myself," Haven continued, "It wasn't easy for me either. My thoughts of you were the best part of my life. They helped my mind escape the nightmare I was in. But when I started to feel like I was never going to make it out of there, I couldn't afford to destroy myself with those thoughts. I couldn't afford to hope. I couldn't afford to imagine. It would just make me weak and make me lose my mind. That's what they would have wanted. I couldn't afford to want anything anymore. I would have given them anything to get that life back and I couldn't afford to betray my country or myself. I couldn't afford to betray you. So, I had to take that away from myself. Forcing myself to stop thinking about you was the hardest thing I had to do, but I had to do it."

Lara shook her head and wiped her tears from her eyes, "I get it." She studied the pages he held in his hand, "So, are you going to publish that?"

He looked down at them, "I was thinking about it."

"I think you should," she encouraged.

"You think," he asked.

She nodded as another question occurred to her, "What do you want to call it?"

He shook his head as he studied his writings, "How about *When You Miss Me?*"

"*When You Miss Me*," Lara said laughing, "That's kind of simple and to the point. Nothing really magical about that."

Haven smiled humbly, "Yeah. That's your dad."

"Hey, I didn't say that," Lara busted out in much-needed laughter.

Haven began laughing as well as he reached to touch his daughter's face. He was the happiest man alive just to have her back in his life.

§

Baroness Coutts: What did you find?

The Mule: Actually, he's squeaky clean.

Baroness Coutts: Not a thing?

The Mule: Well, I didn't say that.

Baroness Coutts: Then what did you say?

The Mule: He has a connection that could appear to be deep state.

Baroness Coutts: Could be or is?

The Mule: Hard to tell.

Baroness Coutts: Can you find out?

The Mule: I can try.

Baroness Coutts: Find out!

The Mule: On it.

§

Casper: Hey buddy ol' pal.

Haven: Hey uh, you?

Casper: Who have you been talking to?

Haven: You will have to be more specific.

Casper: I have a third-rate hacker digging around and he came from your computer. The first thing I'm going to do is give you some information about him so you can know what kind of creepy-crawly things like to wriggle their way through your valuables. Then, I have some software I want you to download ASAP so this never happens again. Keep your battle in your own yard. I don't need it leaking over into my fields.

Haven: I get you big guy. Nice analogy by the way.

Casper: You like that?

Chapter VII

"You have to go through it to get to it."

Dalton roared down a suburban street in his souped-up Nissan Altima his mother had signed for and made most of the payments on to make sure her credit didn't end up like his. It had the nicest discount wheels he could find, and the paint only had a few scratches. But he was proud of his beast. He treated it like his girlfriend even though he didn't have one.

When he took a turn on Jackson Avenue, he started to slow down. The cracks and the potholes bothered him, but it was the only way for him to get home and park in the driveway where he believed his car belonged. If he took the alley behind the house, he had to park in the yard and that just wasn't good enough for him.

He drove past the warehouse and then the eyesore that was his neighbor's house with the old ripped up couch on the porch. He shook his head in disgust as he took another sip of his fast-food soda. Every time he passed that house, that couch was a reminder to him that his life wasn't what it was supposed to be. He was supposed to have been given such a better life than the one he had. He did the best with it is how he reasoned, but the yearning for a much better world was eating at him deeply.

He pulled slowly into the driveway and put it in park. He climbed out of the car in his designer jeans and fashionably ripped sweatshirt. Grabbing his bag of fast food, he then smoothly slid his sunglasses over his eyes before jetting up the three-step entrance to his humble Insulbrick one-level house.

"Is that you Dalton," a lady's raspy voice could be heard coming from the living room.

Dalton put his bag of food on the kitchen counter along with his sunglasses, "Yeah, ma."

"I've been waiting for you," she replied.

"No need to wait for me. Why were you waiting for me?"

"I wanted to see what you wanted for dinner," she responded.

"Oh, I'm good ma. I went to the place down the street and grabbed a few hotdogs," he answered.

He rolled his eyes as he could hear the springs on the couch release as she stood up and came to the entrance. Even though she was in her robe with disheveled brown hair, it was easy to see that she was a very good-looking lady with a few years on her. She looked at him with a serious stare, "You got hotdogs?"

He nodded with slight hesitation, "Yeah."

"I like those hotdogs," she nodded back, "You didn't get your momma one?" She cocked her head with a hard stare.

He cocked his head the other way as his eyes darted around the room before finally catching hers, "No."

She shook her head, "Real good, son. Real good."

"You want a hotdog? I'll go get you a hotdog," he responded in guilt.

"Don't worry about it now. You were there. You didn't think of me then, don't think of me now," she laid it on thick.

He smirked and shook his head, "Mom, I'll go get you a hotdog if you want a hotdog."

She put her hand on her hip and took a few steps into the kitchen, "If you really cared, you would have already done left."

He stood in the middle of the kitchen like he was paralyzed. He didn't know whether to go or not. She had told him not to worry about it, but then she said what she said. If he cared, he would have already left. He was in a dilemma. He couldn't figure his way out of it.

"Don't worry about it, son," she left him off the hook, "I'll whip something up."

"You sure, ma?"

She winced as she rubbed her belly, "Yeah. I just went to the market, Dalton. I've got stuff."

"Oh yeah, what kind of stuff," he asked as his tone changed to a young son being playful.

"Why? What do you want," she asked as she covered her yawn with her hand and then wiped her hair out of her eyes.

"You got spaghetti," he asked curiously.

"You want spaghetti," she responded, "I can do spaghetti."

He walked over to her and gave her a kiss on the cheek before heading out of the kitchen with his food and disappearing down a dark hall. She scratched her back and yawned again as she watched her son vanish into the shadows.

In his dark room with only light from the computer screens, Dalton placed his food beside his monitor in the center of the desk. There were three other monitors above it on a shelf. Each monitor had its own screensaver. But with the simple movement of one mouse, they all sprung back into life at the same time.

Calculations were running on one. Code was showing on another. One monitor had pictures of beautiful women splashed across it while the fourth, the one in the center of the desk was on a forum. Dalton pulled a hotdog out of his bag and then grabbed the fries. He took a big bite of the dog before shoving fries in his mouth. After sucking down some soda, he put the rest of the hotdog down as his attention went to the forum in front of him.

He scrolled through a few headlines until he stopped at one that caught his attention. He studied the headline for a moment as if his face was frozen in time. He shook his head as he clicked on the topic to see what was in it. That's when his life flipped upside down. Not only were the forum members talking about him and they didn't have anything positive to say, but there was a link to an article attached to the post.

His heart sunk as the blood drained from his face. He had made his rather decent living by staying in anonymity. In fact, he made enough money to get his mother out of the humble home they were in and get her into something more like she deserved. But then, he'd have to answer questions. Also, he'd have to give up his lifestyle of doing what he wanted when he wanted and letting his mother take care of everything else on her own.

The anonymity that he had counted on in his pathetic life was suddenly a thing of the past. There before his eyes was his life and where was this information? It was in the last place he ever expected it to be.

Captain Kayd Online

"Exposed: The Mule Is Not Who You Think He Is, But You'll Know Exactly Who He Is Now"

The playboy that many are afraid of, the cyberpunk who built his name off of low-level hacks, has been hiding out at his mom's house where he grew up. He still has the same bedroom. He probably still has the same posters on his wall.

Dalton Connor is almost in his 30s, but he sports around town in his Nissan Altima like a teenager who is still in high school. I bet his mom is so proud. She pays all the bills and even helped buy his car because check this out, Dalton's credit is very, very bad.

That's right, ladies! Stay away unless you want to take the place of his mom. He does not live in that condo many of you think he does. He does not drive that Lambo that you think you've seen him in. In fact, the reality of his life is far, far from that.

Why is he on my radar? He waltzed into my computer like he had any business being there. What was he looking for? What did he find?

I don't know about you folks but when a hacker comes poking around, it comes across to me like I'm onto something. I just may know what I'm talking about and the more I dig, the closer I get to the truth.

But before I get back to that, let's talk about Dalton a little more. He lives at...

As Dalton read the rest of the article, tears started dripping from his eyes. In his world, his anonymity was his power. His mystery was his strength. The Mule was his paycheck, a paycheck that was being shredded to pieces with each new detail The Captain spilled about his life.

As the tears kept streaming, Dalton couldn't help but realize the lesson he had just been taught. He may have started this game, but that was set and match. When you play in a man's world, make sure you know how to play the game.

§

The Practitioner: It's been a long time Baroness.

Baroness Coutts: I know. I wouldn't be coming to you if it wasn't important.

The Practitioner: I saw.

Baroness Coutts: You did?

The Practitioner: You were the one using The Mule, weren't you?

Baroness Coutts: Yes. That was a waste.

The Practitioner: The Mule is good. Or he was good.

Baroness Coutts: Oh yeah? Look what happened to him.

The Practitioner: He definitely barked up the wrong tree. But whose tree is the real question? The Captain is not the tree I'm talking about.

Baroness Coutts: There is someone in deep state.

The Practitioner: There's the tree. So, The Captain is getting help from an insider.

Baroness Coutts: It appears so.

The Practitioner: And you want me to what?

Baroness Coutts: I don't want anything from the deep state guy. Leave that guy alone. I just want The Captain to shut up.

The Practitioner: To shut up about what?

Baroness Coutts: His mission. He can't find out what it was really about. And he doesn't need to be publishing any more details about it on his site.

The Practitioner: That's all you want?

Baroness Coutts: Yes.

The Practitioner: Let me see what I can do.

Baroness Coutts: Thank you!

The Practitioner: Don't thank me. Thank my wallet.

Baroness Coutts: Getting on that now.

§

Geoff Shoerner heard himself snore as his head rested back against his desk chair. He opened his eyes and looked around the room disoriented. After leaning forward and cracking his neck, he looked up at his computer monitor. A yawn forced itself across his face. He grabbed his bottled water and took a drink. Then, he cracked his knuckles and went back to work.

As he typed on the laptop in front of him, the light from the monitor showed the years in the crow's feet around his eyes. He was in his mid-40s, but he looked a little older. He wasn't much for being out in the sun or even seeing daylight. He liked being alone in his dungeon where the outside world became more and more of an illusion to him. It wasn't really a dungeon, but he kept it dark and cool just like one.

An abstract of a man and a child walking down the street hung on the brick wall to his right. It was accompanied by another abstract of an abandoned building. Both paintings were dull in color and lacked straight lines or any specific shape, but they gave themselves to great impressions of their subjects.

In front of him was his headquarters with five monitors controlled by computers on the floor right in front of his feet. His desk had a layer for the monitors in the back to be seen over the monitors in the front. It was quite an elaborate setup, but the only computer he was working on at the time was the laptop in the center.

A huge door opened to the kitchen to his left, a room that doubled as a bedroom as well. His bed was back against the wall within arm's distance of the refrigerator and right by the bathroom door. That was his home. That was all there was to it. Geoff was a simple man who didn't need much more. He thought of his basement apartment as a steal and a place very fitting for himself.

His fingers glided over the laptop keyboard with concise precision. It was like watching the conductor of an orchestra. He gave the laptop a command and it came back lightning fast. With a grin, he gave his laptop a series of other commands and it ran with them. This had been going on for hours, but he was getting close.

He gave the laptop one final set of commands and it started into a rhythmic dance, searching, finding, tracking, and writing data in flawless motion. Geoff leaned back in his desk chair and nodded at his work, "That should hold you for a while." Then, he leaned forward and wiped his forehead. He ran his hand down his face and then looked toward the kitchen.

He stood up with his water bottle and walked toward his bed as he smelled his shirt. Taking it off, he threw it in a chair and pulled open the top drawer of his dresser. Without looking, he grabbed the first shirt he could find and threw it over his head. It was just another dark shirt with sleeves. All of his shirts were dark with sleeves. He had no interest in getting creative with shirts.

He grabbed his wallet and his keys from the top of the dresser and with his water bottle in hand, he headed toward the door. One step outside, Geoff had to squint until his eyes adjusted. He could barely see a thing on such a bright and wonderful day. When the light no longer hurt his eyes, he started up his steps in front of his door until he came to the sidewalk.

He walked with purpose as he headed down the street. People were going in every direction and no one had time to notice each other. He stood out like a sore thumb with his dark shirt, dark jeans, and black leather shoes while everyone else was dressed in business attire. Everyone had a briefcase in their hand and a phone in their ear. Too busy to notice, Geoff walked among them, hiding in plain sight as he made it down the street while the Capitol Building stood proudly behind him.

He caught a quick bite to eat when he grabbed a sandwich at a cozy neighborhood nook. As he finished the last bite of his sandwich, he pulled a small notebook out of his cargo pocket. He looked through a list he had made of the simple words electric, rent, internet, and groceries. He reached back into his cargo pocket for folded up pieces of paper, the bills he had to pay. As he looked through them and marked down how much he had to pay, he tabulated it to be around $1,850 with his electric at almost $300, his rent at $1,200, and his internet at $150 leaving $200 for groceries.

Who sits in a dark two-room apartment with an electric bill of $300? His internet bill even seemed a bit high at $150 when you realize it's just for the internet. There was no television and phone bundle with it. But that was Geoff's business and as he nodded before shoving the bills back in his pocket, it appeared that these were normal for him. His computers and his internet must be working overtime.

As he entered the check cashing store, he approached a clerk who looked as if she knew him very well. She handed him several blank wire transfer forms and waited patiently while he filled them out. She shook her head in amazement as he wrote down routing numbers and account numbers from memory and then handed them back to her. After the transactions went through, she counted out $200 and handed it to him through the window.

That was that. Simple and easy. Everything was done in one place in one flail swoop. He walked away without saying a word. She waved goodbye and as if he could see her behind him, he waved back as he disappeared into the glaring light that hit the glass on the door on his way out.

About an hour later, Geoff arrived home in a car. The driver popped the trunk as Geoff got out of the back seat and grabbed his groceries. The car drove off without saying a word and Geoff carried his bags down the steps to his apartment.

After struggling with the door, he finally entered his apartment with his keys in his mouth. But what he was about to find out was his worse nightmare. His apartment was full of smoke. Geoff dropped the groceries on the floor and looked around to see what was causing all the smoke.

"No! No. No. No. No. No," he said as he ran toward his computers. There they sat, all overheating. Smoke was coming out of the keyboard on his laptop while the screen was literally melting.

§

Captain Kayd Online

"Exposed: The Practitioners Retirement Has Come. Guess Who He Is?"

The loaner who has built a very lucrative hacking business is none other than Geoff Shoerner, another one who was sent after me. Why are they coming? Who is sending them? Now, that has become the question.

He lives in a modest apartment right in the middle of D.C. He pays all his bills through wire transfers from accounts that close shortly after. He has kept his identity confidential because of the people he has worked for. They are the corrupt in our government and they are the people who are behind abandoning a mission that could have saved my life. They were fine with leaving me there to die.

So if that's who he works for and he has no problem taking their blood money, then this is exactly who Geoff Shoerner is...

§

Str8nger: Looks like he's doing pretty good on his own.

The Teacher: He's picked up a few tricks.

Octello: Yeah, but he doesn't know everything yet.

The Teacher: Well, he's just getting started.

Octello: No. I mean there are more pieces to his puzzle.

Str8nger: Like what?

Octello: You're not going to believe this.

The Teacher: Lay it on us.

Octello: I'm working on getting a message through to him. I'll fill you in.

As Haven sat at an outside table at The Marker, a tiki bar just off the water, he was sipping on a Baha Bucket, a tasty drink with several flavors mixed in it. The sun was slowly setting behind him as boats were sailing by in the distance. In front of him was a guitarist strumming out old tunes and to his left was a pool with several swimmers enjoying the water.

As he looked at the beautiful twenty-year-olds, he thought back through his life. Where had his time gone? He felt old in the crowd that was surrounding him. He felt out of place. He should have found a bar with people more his age, but he wasn't too fond of those anymore. The Marker was one of the first places he used to come to when he was going through flight training. It had a certain nostalgia to it and it was hours away from the base. It was a great place to hide and get away from the military environment that could be a bit too much for him at times.

The young waitress came by and he raised his bucket to order another one. That's when his phone beeped. He pulled it out of his pocket and took a good look at the message. It was sent from an unknown source. There wasn't even a number.

*********: No need to reply Captain and no need to worry.

*********: We are friendly.

*********: We've done some digging and we have information for you.

*********: You should look into your mission more.

*********: The fact is, you were supposed to die.

*********: But you didn't and now you have a lot of people scrambling.

*********: Good job with that by the way. You can say I'm a fan.

*********: I am impressed.

*********: And I can see you've read these messages now. So, I'm sorry I have to do this...

Haven's phone suddenly shut off, and then it rebooted itself. When it came back up, the messages were gone. If Haven hadn't been playing this game, it would have deeply frightened him. But he was getting used to encrypted messages and people hiding behind their keyboards. He knew more now than when he first got started, but he could still be surprised sometimes and the wiping of messages from his phone was quite a shocker.

Chapter VIII

"When you play in a man's world, make sure you know how to play the game."

Casper: You are vicious. Have I created a monster?

Haven: From what I know of The Practitioner, it's only a slight setback.

Casper: So, The Practitioner is Geoff Shoerner?

Haven: He tried to destroy my site.

Casper: Told you that was good software.

Haven: Saved my world. It found a sneaky little virus installing corrupt files in my hosting.

Casper: So, you burned his house down?

Haven: This isn't a game to me.

Casper: Have you learned anything new?

Haven: YEAH! I was supposed to die.

Casper: You've got to be kidding me? How did you find that out?

Haven: I got a message from a friendly.

Casper: Who?

Haven: It was encrypted.

Casper: Be careful. You have no idea who you can trust.

Haven: I know. I don't even know if I can trust you.

Casper: True...

§

Captain Kayd Online

"Exposed: The Real Reason My Equipment Failed"

As I dig deeper and deeper into this mystery, I learn more shocking revelations. It's no longer a story about a man who was left to die in an abandoned POW camp. The fact is that I was supposed to die.

What kind of government sends a man out specifically to die? I would be shocked right now if I hadn't been through so much and if I hadn't learned so much about all of it. Nothing I find out shocks me anymore.

It wasn't just recording equipment. They had put other faulty equipment in my jet. Who does that? Why would they do that?

Hackers are being hired to come after me because I'm onto something. So, what I've been saying is true. That's confirmation! If someone is trying to stop me, then I'm reporting the truth here. The question is, why would they want me dead?

That's the question, isn't it?

After pushing publish, Haven turned slightly in his chair to face the sliding doors. It was a sunny day outside and the light was shining through, spilling across his coffee table and onto his couch. Caught in reflection, the beautiful rays from the sun did brighten his spirits a bit. It helped him remember that he was in fact alive, something he had to keep reminding himself every time he found out newer and darker information.

They wanted him dead, but he was alive. He could be grateful for that, but the thought that he had survived against the odds kept shaking him from the peaceful serenity he was able to find at times. What were the odds? His own government wanted him dead. His airplane was fixed to fail. He was thrown in a POW camp on the other side of the world and he was destined to die any day. What were the odds on that?

Haven looked at his drink and shook the glass. He was ready for another one. He was ready for quite a few more. But before he stood up, both thoughts again shot through his mind at the same time. He was supposed to die, but he was here alive. From out of nowhere came a sound from his soul. It was from the center of pain wherever the body holds it, wherever it can be found. It echoed through his chest and poured out of his mouth before he had a chance to hold it back. It was a pitiful sound as if both a child was crying and a man was screaming at the same time.

He was completely overwhelmed by the fact that he was only alive by the slightest of chances. If a government wanted a man dead, he would be dead. Snipers don't miss when they shoot. Naval ships don't miss when they bomb. How is it that he managed to stay alive when his life was cradled in the very hands of the people who wanted him dead?

While his soul was still pouring out its shriek of pain, his glass crashed to the floor. It broke into several pieces, but Haven hadn't even realized. His lungs weren't empty yet and his soul was still grieving. Once the air was completely out, he bent forward with his head down. His hands shaking and tears dripping from his eyes, he felt a world better.

He needed that release. He had bottled up his true emotions for far too long. He had shown the world his brave face while deep inside, his soul was trembling. His heart was racing and his mind was completely blown away. Something had to give and when it finally did, it gave him the strength to keep going.

He wiped the tears from his eyes as he looked out the glass sliding doors and saw the sun again, "That's right. I am alive. I'm still alive. I'm right here." Then, he looked down at his broken glass, "Well, that's not good."

§

Sarah Fulton tapped her toes as she sat in one of the chairs in the middle of the master bedroom. She could hear her husband approaching, but how long it was actually going to take for him to get there was anyone's guess. He couldn't go to the bathroom without someone following him to either ask a question or whisper some kind of nonsense in his ear. The waiting made her all the more impatient.

When the door finally opened, Sarah perked up and looked at the President strange. In turn, he cocked his head and then approached her with caution after closing the door behind him, "You wanted to see me?"

Sarah nodded her head excitedly and his concerns were confirmed. He wasn't used to getting summoned, especially by his wife. How odd it was that she had sent for him in the middle of the day. What was even odder was the fact that she had sent for him at all. Normally, he was the one who did the summoning.

"Have you seen The Captain's latest," she began.

He looked at her with a strange look, "Captain?"

"You know who I'm talking about," she added.

His eyes squinted as they seemed to be searching her mind, "You mean Kayd?"

"That's exactly who I mean," she confirmed.

"What about him," he asked.

"Your briefings are very annoying," she remarked, "It's a wonder you know anything at all."

The President laughed as he took a seat adjacent to his wife, "I'm sorry that my people don't think Captain Kayd is a national security threat."

"He is saying he was supposed to die on that mission," she reported.

"Well, that's not true," George responded, "The ramblings of a frustrated man. Honey, he spent years in a cell. He lost his wife because she thought he was dead. He's upset. He's lashing out."

"He has millions of people listening to him," she responded, "His ramblings are making headlines."

"Fifteen minutes," George uttered, "He's getting his fifteen minutes."

"His fifteen minutes were up months ago," she answered, "He keeps people interested. His life reads like a soap opera."

"And this is why you wanted to see me right now?"

Sarah studied George's eyes as she thought of what to say, "It bothers me that we saved this man and he's a hero now. He can have anything he wants, anything he needs. But he keeps wanting to turn it all into one big conspiracy theory."

"We saved him," George asked with a hint of sarcasm, "He had to escape that POW camp by himself and he was near death when we found him at the crash site."

Sarah winced as she heard George recount the horror, "It was tragic, yes. But we got him. He's here. He's home now. But he's acting like he's leaking classified information to prove it was all a conspiracy against him."

"And you're mad that he's using his Freedom of Speech to tell his story," George asked.

"No," Sarah shook her head, "I'm wondering where he's getting this information, how he's getting it, and what he's going to come up with next." She looked toward the door and then she looked back at her husband, "I'm sure you have a busy day ahead of you. I have things to do myself."

George looked back at her funny as she stood up from her chair and started toward the door, "Sarah!"

She looked back at him as he stood up and walked toward her, "Yes."

"This really bothers you," he asked.

"No. I guess not," she looked him deep in his eyes, "I'm just wondering why we're not more concerned."

He kissed her, a soft loving kiss. Then, he pulled away, "Not a word of it. Don't worry about a word of it." As he started toward the door, he looked back, "I'll see you at dinner."

She stood in the middle of the room with her arms crossed and one foot in front of the other. She simply nodded as she watched the door close behind him. She was still in deep thought as if her conversation with her husband, the President of the United States, had done very little to comfort her. He was the most powerful man on earth and yet, a retired fighter pilot rambling on his website was getting into her head.

§

Washington Daily

"Captain Haven Kayd Has Been Diagnosed With Serious Mental Issues Since Returning Home"

New York Column

"Mental Issues Are To Blame For The Accusations Captain Kayd Has Been Making As Of Late"

Los Angeles Daily

"Captain Haven Kayd, America's Hero Is Suffering From PTSD And Is Often Delusional"

Haven's eyebrows quivered as he read each headline on his laptop. One of his eyes started twitching as the nerves in his body seemed totally shot. He should've expected it. They had tried everything else. They tried to snoop around his computer for secrets he might have been hiding. Then, they tried to take down his site.

Why wouldn't he expect them to start putting out false information about him? But these sources were credible. How in the world did they get these articles published in the *Washington Daily*, the *New York Column*, and the *Los Angeles Daily*? Don't they check their facts?

Of course, facts like that are hard to check. A person's medical issues are between him and his doctor, besides the fact that these weren't even true. He had never been diagnosed with PTSD or any other mental illness. It was clear to him that the people involved in this scandal had power and could make almost anything happen.

It certainly wasn't fun being at this end of the information war, but everything he was publishing was true. As he steamed over the new level this war had reached, his phone started to ring. It was Monica, right on time.

He looked at the phone and then hesitated to answer, "Hello."

"Hi, Haven," Monica greeted in a soft, conciliatory tone, "How's it going?"

Haven rolled his eyes, "You've been reading the headlines, haven't you?"

"You should have told me you are having these issues," she answered.

"Monica, those headlines aren't true," he stated as simply as he could.

"They're not," she asked confused, "Why would they make up these things about you? Why would anyone want to lie about this kind of stuff?"

"Because I'm getting too close to the truth," Haven answered.

"Haven, these aren't independent newspapers that publish whatever they feel like it. These are respectable papers. You've even been on the news," Monica informed.

"What," Haven asked as he turned on the television and changed the channel until he found a news station.

"Honey, do you have PTSD? Are you delusional like they say," Monica asked with concern.

"No. No, Monica," Haven answered with as much sincerity as he could muster, "How would they have gotten my medical records?"

There was a pause and then Monica continued, "So, you're saying it's all because of these things you've been publishing on your site?"

"Yes," Haven confirmed, "Hackers got into my computer and I had to deal with that. Then, they tried to destroy my site. I had to deal with that. Now, this."

"Well, if that's the case, Haven," Monica said with concern, "Don't you think it's getting a little dangerous?"

Now, that was something Haven couldn't argue against. But, he knew what was going to come next. So, he tried a preemptive strike before the conversation took a wrong turn, "I'm fine. I can take a little bad press."

"I'm sure you can," Monica agreed, "But what about the rest of us? What about your daughter?"

Haven had to stop and think about that. Of course, he didn't want anything to happen to his daughter. If they were prepared to start spreading lies about him, would they stoop so low to spread lies about her? Would they stoop so low as to attack her at all? It was time for him to realize that he wasn't the only person who existed in his little world.

It was as if Monica could hear him thinking, "Haven, you're alive. You have a lot of life to live yet. Can't you just move on and enjoy this second chance you've been given?"

With a heavy sigh, Haven answered, "Yeah, I guess I can do that."

"So, you'll stop writing these things," Monica asked.

Again, Haven answered with a heavy sigh, "I'll stop."

Chapter IX

"A bond they felt so strongly, but were afraid to lose again."

Henry listened as the female on the other end of the line ranted on about the pilot who was getting on her last nerve. Henry was a huge fellow with a beard covering his strong jawline. He had a scar on the side of his right eye and his face twitched every so often.

All he needed to know was what she wanted, but he knew to let her get it all off her chest and not interrupt. He could hear something that sounded like glass smashing in the background. Henry simply tilted his head with his phone in his ear and let out a deep breath.

"He's getting too close. I don't know how he's getting his information," the voice screamed. Then, she calmed down and there was a pause.

That was Henry's chance, "So, what do you need me to do?"

"You know what I want you to do," the voice fired back.

Henry sighed as he looked out of his living room window at the tree he had planted himself quite a few years ago, "This is a high profile guy. It will not go unnoticed."

"It will send a message," she responded, "And since when are you in any position to say no to me?"

Henry held the phone away from his ear and then ended the phone call. He looked at the floor until his daughter came running down the steps. She jumped in his lap, "Play with me, daddy!"

"What do you want to play," he asked.

"I made up a new game. You have to find me," she answered.

"I think I know that game," he joked.

"No. It's different. It's a different game," she shot back.

"Okay. So you're going to go hide, right," he asked.

"Yeah, and then you come and find me," she answered.

"Yeah, that sounds a lot like another game I know," he joked.

"No. It's different. Completely different," she said as she ran off giggling and started looking for a hiding place.

Sarah's assistant opened the door and looked into her office, "Ma'am, B.A.H. is here. Your meeting is in about five minutes." As she looked around the room, she saw broken glass on the floor, "Are you okay?"

Sarah had her hand on her phone and was staring off into space until she looked over with half her attention, "What's that?"

"The glass on the floor. Are you okay?"

Sarah looked at it and then back at her assistant, "Oh yeah, I'm fine. It's fine."

"I'll get someone to clean it up. Your meeting is about to start."

Sarah looked at her strange, "What meeting?"

"You have the Bikers Against Homelessness in a few minutes," she answered.

"Oh. Okay. I'll be right there," Sarah stood up and straightened her dress suit.

Her assistant nodded as she closed the door behind her. Sarah picked up her phone and put it on Airplane Mode before putting it in her pocket. Then, she straightened her suit out again before walking out from behind her desk.

§

Haven decided what was best for himself for a while would be a good detox. He needed to get his mind off the scandal and anything related to it. He needed to unwind and find something else to do with his time. So, he filled the gas tank and headed North. He didn't even have a destiny in mind. Once Haven hit I-95 and found himself driving through Daytona Beach, that's when he knew he was just going to sit back and enjoy a long trip.

He must have been thinking subconsciously because he had camping gear in the back of his SUV. It had been there for weeks, but it was about to come in handy. At any given moment, he was ready to fold up the rear seats and blow up the mattress. He had also mapped out various truck stops along the way where he could get a shower and change his clothes.

As he headed up the coast driving through St. Augustine and then through Jacksonville, the smile on his soul got wider and wider. But circling still were many thoughts fresh on his mind. It's hard to simply detox after a few hours of driving. It was going to take a while.

The night had already fallen by the time he drove into Georgia heading toward Savannah. That was the time Haven enjoyed driving the most when everyone else was off the road and it felt like just him and his Honda CR-V. All the missions he had ever gone on in his life were just him and his equipment out there on their own.

And just like that, his mind slipped from enjoying the quiet serenity of the road to memories of his equipment failure on that flight over Afghanistan. His heart rate increased and his breathing turned heavy as the road in front of him disappeared into a dark sky and his dash turned into a cockpit with flashing lights indicating equipment failure. He could see the ground in front of him quickly approaching as he reached for his ejector seat. His hand would find nothing there as it kept feeling around in the area where it was supposed to be.

Then, Haven came back to his senses. He was driving on I-95. He wasn't back in his jet. His eyes darted around on the road as his breathing, still heavy, was starting to calm after taking in a few deep breaths. His heart rate eventually returned to normal as he found himself crossing Lake Marion, a beautiful expanse of water that could bring back anyone's peace.

The sleepy lake was coming awake as houselights lit the bank on the far side and the morning light was rising in the distance. He had been driving all night and somehow missed Savannah on his way out of Georgia. He shook off those old memories. That's what the trip was about, to get away from those thoughts and start to take on new ones.

The flashbacks and the mind-gripping thoughts of the scandal started to fade with each city he encountered along the way. He was focusing more on the trip and learning to truly leave those things behind him, at least for the moment as he enjoyed the drive through Fayetteville, North Carolina on his way to the small town of Rocky Mount. He could see the smokestacks and the abandoned buildings of the various industries that had shut down years before and he could almost tell the history of the people leaving to find work while others stayed to pick up the pieces. It reminded him of another town up North.

Cumberland, Maryland was much like Rocky Mount. The industries had all moved out to find better tax and property deals in other states, leaving an entire town to struggle with the heartless changes that faceless corporations impose on them with the false hope they bring. Small rural areas that build themselves on promises and grow to rely on the boom these companies bring until one day, the brand packs up and moves away leaving people without jobs and small businesses without paying customers.

As Haven watched the buildings of Rocky Mount pass by, he realized one destination he could put in his GPS. He hadn't been to Cumberland for a long, long time. It might do him some good to catch up with people he hadn't seen for years. But he was starting to get hungry and that reminded him of another place. He knew where he wanted to eat and it was only a few more hours up the road.

He was trying to remember where the diner was as he came off of U.S. Route 1 before turning onto Williams Street heading toward downtown Fredericksburg, Virginia. He was working on pure instinct as Williams Street took him to Caroline and he knew to take a left. That's when it all came rushing back to him. Driving along Caroline, he was reacquainted with the Rappahannock River, an old friend of his he had known since his youth when he used to body surf it back in the day.

As Caroline took him to Old Mill Park, again his instincts took over and he took a left on Germania. One block up and he found it on his right. With a sign that reads "Let's Eat" and the words "Family Restaurant" written on the siding of the roof, Haven knew he had finally reached his destination.

He stepped out of the SUV and stretched his legs as he studied the diner and cracked his back. He cocked his head as he looked it over from the outside. It was definitely familiar to him, but something was different. When he stepped inside, he shook his head with a wince on his face. The diner was not as big as he remembered it to be.

Of course, the last time he had stepped in the diner was when he was in high school. Even at that age, time can change a man's perspective of the world around him. It doesn't take being a toddler to imagine that the seats were taller and the aisle was wider than what they actually were.

A quaint diner nonetheless, Haven looked around and found a seat at the end of the counter. The waitress was in front of him with a pot of coffee and a clean cup before he had a chance to sit down. Coffee wasn't at all what he needed when all he was going to do after eating was check into a hotel and hit the bed faster than his clothes could hit the floor. But the coffee was already poured and he didn't even think to object. He simply started adding sugar and cream as the waitress handed him a menu while pointing out the specials.

Nothing like an omelet and an order of hash browns to fill his stomach after driving all night and most of the day. He took his time eating while he looked around. As much as the world had changed over the years, this diner was pretty much still the same. Same pictures on the wall. Same cash register that should have been updated years ago. Same seats. In fact, the same leather that only years of wear had changed.

But what caught his eye the most was the father and daughter sitting in the booth a few feet away from him. At least, he thought they were father and daughter until he overheard her talking to the man about her father. An odd man with odd ideas who taught his daughter to shoot at an early age and then, he hired her to drive moonshine for him when he took on a job with Animal Control. It was cute how she referred to him as an animal catcher.

Haven shook his head. Who would send their daughter out to deliver moonshine? Then, he realized where he was. He had grown up in these parts and yes, that's part of the Virginia world. Take a wrong turn around here and you can easily end up in the Appalachian Mountains with a shotgun in your face.

Haven didn't mean to hear that much of their conversation, but she was talking a little loud and in this particular diner, it was easy to hear. Listening to her tell stories about her father made him think of his own daughter and all the time he had missed with her. He missed out on all those years, things they could have done together.

His mind went off into complete oblivion as he imagined taking his daughter to a fair. They played games and rode rides, always a smile on her face and her laugh. It echoed in his mind as he watched her eat cotton candy and then, she was walking in front of him. She looked back and her hair whipped around. His imagination put a smile on his soul. It was as if they were actually there.

That's when a look came over her face that changed what his soul was feeling. She looked over at a game as a tear fell out of her eye. When he looked, he could see the lights flashing and the sound kept playing over and over. It was a familiar sound that snapped him out of his daydream and back into reality.

When he looked down at his phone, it was Monica. He looked at it with a strange expression and immediately, his heart felt heavy. When he picked it up, he heard her voice on the other end of the line and his heart dropped as his body began to shake, "Haven, Lara is missing!"

"What do you mean she's missing," Haven asked, his heart racing and his mind going a million miles a second.

"She didn't come home last night," Monica answered.

Haven threw money down on the counter and nodded abruptly to the waitress as he hustled out of the diner. Once outside, he asked, "Where was she supposed to be?"

Monica answered, "At the fair with her friends!"

Haven's mind went numb. He quickly flashed back to his daydream of his daughter's sad face at the fair and he couldn't shake how uncanny that was.

But he had little time to think about it as Monica had raised her voice a few octaves, "What were you thinking?"

"What are you talking about?"

"I thought you made a promise you would stop publishing articles on your site," she asked.

"I did," he answered.

"Well then, why is there another article," she asked, "And it says some pretty far-out stuff. You promised!"

He could hear her crying on the other end of the line, "What are you talking about?"

"The article," she said in a whimper.

"Look! I'm on my way," Haven said before shutting off the phone call as he made his way to his SUV.

He jumped in and started it up while he looked for his site on the phone. He couldn't believe his eyes. There it was, a new article, "What? I didn't write that!"

He pulled out of the parking lot squealing wheels on his way back to Florida. Dead tired and only one meal in him, he flew back down I-95 without a second thought. His mind burned from lack of sleep and the worst thoughts in the world racing with every mile he drove. But nothing was going to keep him from finding out where his daughter was and he was pretty sure he knew what had happened to her.

Captain Kayd Online

"Exposed: The Reason I Was Supposed To Die"

The Captain's scandal keeps growing. Yes, he was in a POW camp and yes, he was supposed to die. Why would our own government want him dead? That's a long and arduous story. So, I'll make it short.

The deep state that exists within our government wanted him dead to be a poster boy for a new contract deal. New planes were on the list of items this fairly new company made, but there's more to it than that. This company would allow these deep state individuals to funnel money.

But the more important part of the story is why they wanted to funnel money. Did they want to finance wars? Did they want to pad their own pockets?

The answer is that they wanted to pad their own pockets but in the most coldblooded way. The money they would be able to funnel would go to financing human trafficking...

Chapter X

"Evil knows what it's doing is evil. Don't expect it to change because of your cute Self-Improvement quotes."

When Haven arrived in Clearwater sixteen hours later, the first place he went was the fair. He didn't have time to deal with Monica and he didn't have time to think about how exhausted he was. Another thing he didn't have time to do was worry about his website, why it was hacked, or what else was being published on it.

If anything, he thought it would be a good idea to just let it go. It seemed that it could serve as a good roadmap for him if what was being published was true and if friendlies were informing him of the deeper secrets that he was unable to find himself.

As he looked around the fairgrounds, it felt hopeless. The fair had packed up and left. What was left behind was nothing but trash that a few workers were cleaning. There was too much ground to cover and that's about the moment when he realized that he was no detective. Thinking about that made him realize something else. He had a resource. He pulled his phone out of his pocket and dialed.

"Hey! Long time no see," he heard Carlos say on the other end of the line.

"Uh yeah detective, I don't really have much time for small talk," Haven replied.

"Oh," Carlos said with an alarming voice, "What uh, what do you need?"

"I think my daughter has been kidnapped and I need your help," Haven spilled as quickly as he could.

"What," Carlos said with instant worry, "Why do you think that?"

"I don't have time to go into the whole thing. I need you to tell me what to do next," Haven answered quickly.

"Uh Haven, I'm retired now," Carlos paused, "But, let's see. Where is the last place you know where she was?"

"Oh, congratulations," Haven said, and then without skipping a beat, "I don't need you to do anything. Just help me. I'm ahead of you on that. I'm at the fairgrounds."

"She was at the fair," Carlos started calculating, "That's tough. That's a big place. Lots of people."

"Actually, it's shut down," Haven further informed, "There are people cleaning up the mess. That's about it."

Carlos did his best to turn on his detective mind with as little information as he had and it clicked, "Look around for video cameras."

Haven looked around the area and there was nothing in sight. Possibly if he looked hard enough, he could find something. But no cigar, "There are no cameras here."

"Then, you have to chase the fair. They have the cameras and most likely still have the footage," Carlos said.

"Okay. Can you do me a favor and chase down the fair? Let me know where it's going," Haven commanded.

"On it," Carlos answered, "Sit tight."

§

Haven had no idea how long it was going to take Carlos, so he headed to his apartment in the meantime. He didn't know how much sleep he was going to be able to squeeze into his short visit home, but there was another reason he needed to be heading there. If what he feared was true, he knew he couldn't go in empty-handed.

It didn't take Carlos long to find out that The Big Umbrella was the moving fair that had been in Largo and was heading North to Jacksonville. But Haven wasn't going to have to drive there. Carlos had the company forward him the footage and he went through four hours of video to find Haven's daughter.

He gritted his teeth and his entire body tensed up. The urge to kill someone shot through every muscle. Then, he sat back and took in a few deep breaths. He copied off a picture of the three guys who grabbed her and threw her into a black SUV before squealing out of the fairgrounds. He texted a copy to Haven and then, he went to work.

His fingers were lightning fast as he did something he was no longer authorized to do since he had finally retired. He entered the California State Police database and started running their facial recognition software. That's when he heard his phone start ringing.

He answered, "Calm down! The only thing to do is remain calm. I'm going to find out who these guys are. You stay put and don't make a move until you get my call."

Haven didn't even have time to ask any questions or to freak out. But Carlos could hear it in his trembling voice, "Just...just stay put? I have to find her."

"And that's exactly what I'm trying to do, as fast as I can. It does you no good running off in any direction. Just stay put!"

While Carlos was trying to talk Haven down from a nervous breakdown, he was watching the computer as it ran checks through thousands of criminals. In the time Carlos had known Haven, he knew what kind of man he was. If something needed to be done, he was going to do it himself. Plus, Carlos knew that if the cops got involved, they'd follow a certain protocol. Even with the photo as evidence, the police would still move at a steady pace because they have to make sure everything they do is by the book. Let alone, Carlos was quite aware of how many felonies he had committed already.

So, the book was thrown out the window. Carlos was in and he was in deep at this point. The sad part was, the criminal database search came up empty. There was no positive identification on either of the men. He scratched his head as the wheels kept turning in his mind. Then, he started typing again.

§

Str8nger: The game just got more interesting.

The Teacher: Why? What happened?

Octello: What's new?

St8nger: I intercepted a text. The Captain's daughter's been kidnapped.

Octello: By who?

Str8nger: I'll send the photo.

The Teacher: How did you get that?

Str8nger: Looks like The Captain has a detective friend in L.A.

Octello: I'll start running their faces, beginning with the National Driver Register.

Str8nger: Don't you think the detective is already doing that?

Octello: We'll have it first.

Str8nger: Okay. I'll post an update on the website.

The Teacher: Do we have an unfair advantage?

Octello: Haven has an unfair disadvantage...

Str8nger: Right on.

The Teacher: Well said. Game on.

Octello: Game on.

§

Haven woke up on the couch to the phone ringing. He jumped up and answered it before even looking at it. Who he heard on the other end was not who he expected, "You know who the people are and you didn't think to contact me?"

"Monica, slow down. What," Haven tried to quickly pull himself out of a deep sleep and gain his senses again, "What?"

"Why do you keep acting like you don't know what I'm talking about," Monica fired back, "You published another article on your website!"

"Uh Monica," Haven shook his head as he couldn't believe the words that were about to come out of his own mouth, "I haven't been publishing those. I don't know what article you're talking about."

"You're trying to tell me that you're not publishing the articles on your own site," Monica asked skeptically.

"Yes. That's what I'm saying," Haven answered and then hesitated, "Look. Some hackers have taken over my website and they published the one about human trafficking. Now if they've published something new, I have to read it."

"You what," Monica yelled, "You're going to go and read your website now?"

"Yes," Haven answered, "It could help me find her!"

Monica started crying, "I knew it. I knew something was wrong. I had this feeling something like this had happened. I called a hundred times. I left messages. She always answers."

"Listen," Haven swallowed hard and said anxiously, "I'm going to find her. She's going to be fine."

"The cops are already involved," Monica informed, "And they have no idea where she is. How are you going to do more than they can?"

"Because I'm not going to stand in my own way," Haven answered.

"What is that even supposed to mean," Monica asked.

"It means, I don't have to follow their rules," Haven answered, "I'm going to find her and bring her back to you. I promise."

Haven could hear Monica breathing heavily and he could almost feel the tears dropping from her eyes. But he was not ready for Monica's next words, "When this over, you are never going to see your daughter again."

"Monica? Monica," Haven kept asking. But the line was dead. She had hung up and left him with that terrible feeling in the pit of his stomach, but he didn't have time to think about Monica's threats. He had to find out what was new on his website and if it meant anything.

Captain Kayd Online

"The Captain's Scandal Has Escalated And This Is As Low As It Gets"

Of course, The Captain was onto the truth. He got so close in fact, they have retaliated in the worst possible way. They sent three guys to kidnap his daughter and where they're heading is anyone's guess. But we plan on following them every step of the way.

First of all, let's talk about who these guys are...

The article was very informative about the men it outlined as Henry, Art, and Rip. The feature image of course was the photo of her being abducted by the three men. Then, there was a profile paragraph accompanied by a driver's license photo for each of the monsters.

Of course, Henry was the bearded one with the scar by his right eye. What was disturbing was his military background. He was Army Special Forces with an Honorable Discharge and absolutely no criminal record. For Haven, it was a particularly bitter sting that one of his own, someone who had served, was in on the abduction of his daughter. It can be expected of the scum of the earth. But when it's someone who is supposed to be one of the good guys, it's a harsh pill to swallow.

Art was another guy with absolutely no record. Haven was starting to see a pattern. How high up it went, he had no idea. But they either chose very clean men or they kept them clean somehow while these guys did the dirty jobs no one else dared to touch. Art's photo looked like he had just come straight from teaching a college class with his impossible sandy blond hair and clean-shaven face. But he had some size to him. There was no denying that.

There was no surprise that Rip's record was clean as well. What stood out about Rip was the fact that he looked like the serious thug among them. His hair hung over his face in the abduction photo. But on his driver's license, his curly brown hair was tied behind his head and his eyes were hypnotically wild. No scars, no tattoos, and no smile. Just those wild eyes that could penetrate a person's soul.

"What have I gotten my daughter into," Haven said to himself with a shaky voice.

§

Lara was steady staring out the window with tears rolling down her cheeks. She was trying her best to be quiet, but she couldn't stop the tears. She looked down at her hands cuffed with a zip tie and shook her head in confusion with more tears falling from her eyes. Then, she took a quick look at the men around her.

She was trying her best to notice every detail and to remember as many landmarks as she could find along the highway. But she felt hopeless at this point. They had taken her phone and threw it in a bag on the floor in the front seat.

She had no idea where she was going or why. She didn't even know what day it was. It felt like only a few hours ago that she was at the fair having a good time with some friends. It all happened so fast how she was grabbed and then, she was gone. She could see her friends looking around for her as the SUV drove her further and further away from safety.

She put her hands to her face and tried to hold back from crying. Henry looked around at her and shook his head, "Don't worry. It's not that long of a ride. If you don't try anything, nothing will happen to you and you won't see us anymore."

Sitting in the back with her, Rip shot her a sideways glance, "Yeah, just don't try anything. That's the main thing."

Lara looked over at him with her red tear-filled eyes. He crossed his arms and raised an eyebrow without even a sign of feelings. Henry tightened his lips with a slight wince of humanity in his eye, and then he turned around to face forward.

Frightened beyond belief, the most awful feeling lingered in the pit of her stomach. She looked at Henry and then back at Rip, the most terrifying glare a child should never have to see even in her worst nightmare. She quickly turned to her window again to hide her face and the many tears she simply couldn't manage to stop.

Meanwhile, deep down in the bag on the floor in the front seat, her phone lit up. The volume went to mute and software began downloading as if by itself. Then, the light on the screen went off and the phone went back to sleep.

§

The Teacher: Okay. I just installed a tracker on her phone. Sharing GPS now.

Octello: Can we duplicate that on their phones?

The Teacher: Good idea. I'll see.

Str8nger: I already took care of it.

Octello: Really? How? Just curious.

Str8nger: I pinged all the phones in her immediate vicinity.

Octello: lol

The Teacher: Good thinking.

Octello: I love this game!

Chapter XI

"You know you're going to get brain freeze, but you keep eating the ice cream anyway..."

When Haven received a location report from an anonymous sender, he wanted to grab his things and rush out the door. But then, he stopped to think about it for a moment. Was he being helped by friendly hackers or was the other side trying to send him into a trap?

It started with confusion when Carlos sent him driver's license pictures of the three men who had abducted his daughter. Haven called him immediately, "Carlos, have you been hacking my website?"

"Uh no, I'm not a hacker," Carlos answered surprised.

"You're not a hacker," Haven asked with an even more suspicious tone.

"I am not," Carlos confirmed, "Why do you keep asking?"

"Have you seen my site," Haven asked.

Carlos paused for a moment, "Give me a second." Carlos pulled up Haven's site and there they were, the same photos he had just sent. "I don't know what's going on here. But I did not hack your site, man."

Haven took a moment and tried to think it through. It seemed Carlos was trying to help. If he was a part of this for any reason, would he try to help? To lead him away in the opposite direction? Haven thought of a test and possibly a way to make sure, "Do you know where they are?"

"All I was able to do was find out who they are," Carlos answered, "I have no way of tracking them down or knowing where they're headed. I'm sorry, buddy."

Haven looked down at his phone with a photo of the map with a pin at the last known location. If Carlos was trying to lead him away, he would have tried. He would have lied, but he didn't, "Okay, Carlos. Sorry man. My site's been hacked with these articles I didn't publish and it just gets hard to figure out or to know..."

Carlos interrupted him before he had a chance to say it, "I know, man. You don't have to say it. I wouldn't know who to trust either at this point. I wish I could do more for you. If I come up with something, I will."

Haven nodded, "Thanks, man."

"No problem," Carlos replied, "I hope it helps. I hope..." He stopped himself. He knew he couldn't promise Haven anything and he knew empty words weren't going to do any good.

"I know," Haven said, "I have to go."

§

Haven made good time to Enterprise, Alabama, the last known location of his daughter. He pulled up at a café along Main Street and with a moment to think about things, he looked at his watch and then counted backward. The timeframe didn't quite make sense.

It took him seven hours to get to Enterprise from Clearwater. So by some kind of crazy algorithm Haven had no idea how to calculate, they were only seven hours ahead of him and he had no idea what direction they were going. He was hoping, with big faith in a very blind hope that someone soon would let him know something somehow.

But it was a different timeline that really had him baffled. He was in Fredericksburg, Virginia when he learned about his daughter's abduction. That was almost two days ago, and the abductors had only made it seven hours up the road? They were going unbelievably slow. Maybe they stayed in a hotel for a day. Maybe they were in no hurry. Whatever was slowing them down, it was working to Haven's benefit.

Haven looked at his phone in frustration and then, he looked at the café in front of him. Grabbing something to eat wouldn't be such a bad idea. A big cup of coffee wouldn't hurt either. If he got back from the café and hadn't received any updates, he was going to have to start trying to figure things out on his own.

§

Just off of I-10 in Breaux Bridge, Louisiana, Henry pointed out a Rodeway Inn tucked behind a small car dealership and an out-of-business gas station. With only two cars in the entire parking lot, it looked like a ghost town. Henry nodded his head. It was perfect.

Rip stretched his back and cracked his neck, "The third hotel room in two days. What's the deal?"

Henry looked around at Rip and then at Lara, "Well for one, I don't know where we're going yet. They haven't given me the destination."

Rip looked over at Lara, "So, we're just highly paid babysitters for now."

Henry nodded and then looked forward again, "Pretty much."

Art put the SUV in park at the office, "Okay, I'll go get the room. Are we grabbing food anywhere or is it a bag of noodles again?"

With a surprising hint of humanity, Rip offered, "I don't know about the girl, but I could go for a good cheeseburger." Lara shot him a glance and saw him eyeing her, "Cheeseburger sounds good, right?"

Lara gave it a thought and then nodded thankfully. Henry caught the exchange between the two, "Okay. I'll get us something after we get in the room."

§

Octello: The Captain is in Enterprise.

The Teacher: What? He is a hero. He's going after them himself.

Str8nger: You didn't expect him to chase?

The Teacher: I wouldn't have. I would have told the cops where they were.

Octello: The Captain is made of different stuff.

Str8nger: The Right Stuff.

The Teacher: They were astronauts.

Str8nger: They were all fighter pilots first.

The Teacher: Fair enough.

Octello: Good point.

The Teacher: Okay. If he's going to chase them down, let's give him everything we have.

Octello: We've got the license plate number from the abduction footage.

Str8nger: I have them currently at a Rodeway Inn in Louisiana with confirmation of her life.

The Teacher: So, The Captain is about six and a half hours away. He might be able to catch up. From here on out, let's get all the footage we can from traffic lights to gas station cameras and everything else in between.

§

Baroness Coutts: Is this urgent?

The Fuse: I think it is.

Baroness Coutts: What is it then?

The Fuse: The Captain has recruited help.

Baroness Coutts: What help?

The Fuse: Some of the best in the business.

Baroness Coutts: Shut them down!

The Fuse: I repeat the part about the best in the business.

Baroness Coutts: How are they helping him?

The Fuse: Tracking his daughter down.

Baroness Coutts: They're not trying to dig anymore.

The Fuse: I'm pretty sure what's out there is all there is to the story.

Baroness Coutts: You have no idea.

The Fuse: What would you like me to do?

The Fuse: ?

The Fuse: ???

Baroness Coutts: Just keep muddying the water.

In the bedroom the President shared with the First Lady in the White House, Sarah turned away from her laptop. Tapping a pen on the desk, the wheels in her mind were turning. How bad was this going to get?

News of the abduction was already on every channel. If Henry and his men weren't aware of that, it was their own fault. That's part of their job to be aware of the dangers. She felt no need to contact them any further. Each communication was risky.

After all, Lara's buyers were already on their way to Truth or Consequences, New Mexico. It was in their hands to communicate with Henry the location of the meeting. Sarah could keep her hands clean from here on out, or at least not dirty them any further.

§

"He needs to get back with that food soon," Art said as he flipped the channels on the television.

Lara was sitting on the bed with her back against the headboard and her knees to her chest. Her mind was racing through the worst she could imagine. What were they going to do with her? She had heard of girls her age and younger coming up missing. Her heart felt heavy every time the thought of it raced through her mind.

Rip yawned as he looked at his phone. He was thinking of calling Henry to find out where he was and how long it was going to take. But the more he looked at his phone, it was as if his brain had shut off completely and he had forgotten what he wanted it for in the first place. He was having that kind of day.

In a dark room on the other side of the country, a mysterious lady monitored her desktop. Rip's face was on her screen. He was so close to the camera, she could count his nose hairs. She watched him for a few more moments and then began typing.

Octello: Lara's still fine. She's holding up. This Rip guy needs some hygiene though.

The Teacher: Good looking out.

As Art kept flipping the channels, he suddenly saw himself. On the television just a few feet away from him was his driver's license photo. Then, the news story showed Rip's driver's license photo and Henry's after that. As the reporter kept talking, footage of the abduction was played on a loop.

"The girl being abducted is Lara Kayd, the daughter of Captain Haven Kayd, the Marine Corps pilot who survived years in a POW camp and earned instant notoriety after his amazing escape. If you have seen these men or know anything about their whereabouts, you can call your local law enforcement agency and report what you know. Any detail whether you think it is big or small can help find Lara, so don't hesitate to call your local law enforcement agency if you know anything at all..."

Rip was steadily staring at the television, his nostrils flaring with each breath he took. Art's eyes were wide open and his face had turned a shade of pale. Lara tried to be subtle, but she could see a glimmer of hope. It was known that she was abducted and their faces were all over the television. It was just a matter of time for someone to spot them and that gave her the hope she needed.

Suddenly, Henry busted through the door with bags of food and startled everyone. The looks he got from both Rip and Art were enough to set off warning signals in his head, "What?"

"We're all over the news," Art started, "They have our faces and our names all over the news."

"How," Henry asked.

"They have footage at the fair," Rip chimed in, "They got our driver's license photos from that."

Henry looked at the television, but the news story had changed to the weather. He threw the food on the table and carefully looked out the window. The parking lot was bare except for their SUV. He looked up toward the entrance and couldn't see anything suspicious, "We are fine here for now. I'll try to push things up. But I can't let them think in any way that we've lost control of the situation. So, let's just sit tight."

Lara looked up at the ceiling. Her thoughts of hope faded with the words she just heard come out of Henry's mouth. They had a plan for her and she had no idea what it was. Her mind started racing through the worst-case scenarios again.

Chapter XII

"Our lives are nothing but a bet cosmic gamblers made a long time ago just to pass the time."

New York Column

"Haven Kayd Is Wanted By The FBI For Leaking Confidential Information He Obtained Illegally"

Washington Daily

"Haven Kayd's Lies Have Put A Lot Of People's Lives In Danger, Including His Daughter's"

Los Angeles Daily

"The FBI Is Searching For Haven Kayd For His Involvement In His Daughter's Disappearance"

Haven crept up Frontage Road past a truck rental on his left. He could see the hotel through the trees. As he pulled past the abandoned gas station, he pulled into the car dealership where he got a much better look at the hotel. There it was, the SUV he had been chasing.

Haven could feel his blood pressure rising and a tightening in his chest, but he knew he had to keep his emotions in check. All he wanted to do was rush up there, guns blazing. But he knew that could get her killed and he was doing his best to think things through.

He looked back at the road he had just come down. That's when a thought occurred to him. He backed up and then headed back to the abandoned gas station. There was a clearing through the line of trees that went to the hotel parking lot on the backside of the hotel. If he crept through, he could drive around to the other end of the hotel, and then he'd be closer to the situation.

That would give him a chance to be hidden, but near. From there, he'd just have to hope for an opportunity. He thought about simply calling the police and letting them know where the kidnappers were, but then he realized that could put her in more danger.

These guys were well connected somehow. He knew that. What if those connections could interfere with a hostage situation? Haven couldn't take that chance. This was his opportunity to get her back alive and if anyone was going to care about the girl inside that hotel room, Haven knew he couldn't trust it to anyone else but himself.

He thought of rushing in the room and shooting every one of them with one shot, and then he got realistic. Knowing him, he'd trip on the way into the room. Or he'd miss every shot and end up full of bullets himself. But the scenario of him rushing into the room kept running through his mind because if he was any greater of a man, he would have already done it by now.

As it was, he was parked at the end of the hotel with eyes on the SUV. He was hidden just beyond the corner of the building so that he could keep an eye on them while they had no idea he was there. At least, he knew that much.

But as far as the rest of it was concerned, he had no idea what he was going to do. He was up against a guy with special forces training and who knew what the other two were capable of doing. The unfortunate part about it, he was about to find out. He knew the time to act was only a few short moments away.

With no plan and no warning, he was unprepared when he saw Henry come out of the room in the early morning hours just before sunrise and throw his bag in the back of the SUV. He jumped in the front and started it up as it looked like he was taking a moment to go through his phone. This was it! This was time for Haven to figure out what he was going to do.

He started his SUV and drove around the backside of the hotel to the office where he could get a view of their room door. When he watched Rip and Art bring their bags out to the SUV, he waited patiently until they went back into the room. By this time, Henry had already gone back inside himself. So, Haven drove as quietly as he could and got as close as possible.

As the men came out of the room, Rip and Art led while Henry tried nonchalantly to walk Lara to the SUV. They all spotted Haven's vehicle at the same time and froze in place. They pulled out their guns and started looking around, but Haven made his move before they got a chance to see him.

Coming up from behind, Haven pressed his gun to Henry's head and grabbed his arm, "Let her go!"

Henry did as he was told, but the other two were now pointing their guns at Haven. Lara was stiff as a board, paralyzed as to what to do. Henry decided to break the tension, "Ah, Daddy came to save the day!"

"Lara, get in the car," Haven ordered.

"She's not going anywhere, pal," Rip informed.

"Let her go or he gets one in the head," Haven responded.

"I don't care," Rip gave an unsuspected answer, "Less ways to split the money."

"You don't care," Haven asked astonished. Change of plans, "Lara, get behind me."

Lara walked softly around Henry and her father. Her heart was beating fast, but she was safe. She felt so safe at that moment that all the terrible thoughts that had been running through her mind since her abduction suddenly disappeared. Haven led the way with his gun pointed at Henry's head. He made sure to keep Henry between Rip and himself. Then he looked at Art, and with the wave of his gun, he directed Art to get over with Rip.

Art slowly nodded his head and started moving as he watched Haven creep closer and closer to his SUV. When he had finally circled around and backed up to the SUV, Haven told Lara, "Get in the car."

Lara backed up until she was behind the SUV, and then she ran around to the passenger side. Rip started to move in that direction, but Haven warned him, "Ah ah ah, don't move!"

Then, in a split-second decision, Haven butted Henry on the head with the pistol grip and jumped in the driver's seat. He put it in gear and took off as fast as he could. Rip and Art immediately returned fire, but they only hit the side of the SUV as Haven drove off toward the backside of the hotel. He turned the corner and was out of sight while Henry was picking himself up from the parking lot, "Get in!"

As Haven drove around the hotel to get back to the exit, he could feel pain in his side. He looked down and could see that he had been hit, but he had no time to worry about that at the moment and he didn't want to alarm his daughter. So, he kept driving as fast as he could. As he rounded the front of the hotel, he could see their SUV waiting for him.

He looked at the exit they were blocking and then, he remembered the way he came. He slid sideways and hit the gas to turn into the clearing through the trees. As he shot through, his SUV bounced on every bump. He did his best to steer as they barreled up to Frontage Road, bouncing off the seat and hitting their heads on the roof with every mound in the field.

"Hold on, honey," Haven yelled.

"Dad," was all Lara could scream as she did her best to hold on to anything.

Art was right behind him as he too went through the clearing in the trees and across the field to Frontage Road. He followed as Haven turned and hit the gas. The chase was on as they headed North, Art trying to pass and Haven doing his best to block him. It was a high-speed chase that bound dangerously through crossroads with no concern for any other traffic.

A few close calls so hairy, Haven's heart leapt in his chest and Lara screamed. But nothing was going to get him to slow down, not while Art was steady on his tail. He barreled down the road, not knowing where he was or where he was going. He had to think fast and he had no idea what it was going to take to lose the guys behind him who annoyingly refused to give up.

That's when Art noticed something odd. Haven's SUV was slowing down. It swerved a little and then, it drifted to the center of the road where it finally came to a stop. Art stopped a few feet behind it. Rip jumped out and pulled his gun. Art and Henry followed. They cautiously approached, Rip on one side and the other two on the other.

When they got to the window, they found Haven slumped over in the seat and Lara crying hysterically, "Daddy! Get up! Dad! Daddy!"

Rip reached into the SUV and grabbed Lara. She kicked and screamed, but she was no match for Rip. In the meantime, Henry yanked Haven out of the driver's side and threw him on the ground. Haven woke up momentarily and watched as Rip threw his daughter into the other vehicle. He tried with all his might to get up, but Art swiftly kicked him and Haven again lost consciousness.

Rip transferred his bags to Haven's SUV while Art threw Haven in the back. Henry took off alone with Lara while Art and Rip headed in the opposite direction with the man who had almost ruined their financial plans. With the look on Rip's face, whatever they had in store for Haven wasn't going to be good.

§

Str8nger: That was a wild ride.

The Teacher: GPS indicates speeds up to 120.

Octello: What a shame...

The Teacher: Yeah, he lost the battle but put up a good fight.

Str8nger: I have a shred of hope for him though.

The Teacher: Seriously? You're eaten up. There's no way he gets out of this.

Octello: Sounds like a bet.

The Teacher: I'm down.

Str8nger: It's a bet.

Chapter XIII

"Life is like being in a commercial no one is watching because that's when everyone gets up to go to the bathroom."

Octello: The vehicles split in San Antonio. The lead car is still on I-10W. The other one is heading down I-35S toward Mexico.

The Teacher: The vehicle on I-35 must have The Captain.

Str8nger: I-35S? That's heading toward Mexico. We'll eventually lose sight. I know that area pretty well.

§

When Haven came to, he found himself in the back of his own SUV with Rip in the passenger seat and Art driving. His hands were zip-tied and he was slumped over on the bench seat. Fighting to sit up, a sharp pain shot through his side where his shirt had fused to the bullet hole, a fortunate accident that eventually slowed the bleeding and gave his body a chance to adjust to the shock.

Rip looked around when he heard Haven grunting. Even if Rip's job was to take Haven to Coahuila and bury him in the Chihuahuan Desert, he had to admit that he had respect for the man. He came after his daughter with no hesitation and here he was, still putting up a fight with a bullet hole in his side. Rip might have been a monster, but he had to respect a man that wasn't about to go down like a coward.

Haven shot Rip a look of hatred, a look the man definitely understood. So, he simply nodded and turned his head back around. That's when Haven started to try to figure out where he was. Just as he saw I-35, they passed a gas station and took a right onto a long stretch of road heading nowhere.

§

The Teacher: Well it was fun following you, Captain. That's the end of visual contact.

Str8nger: We still have GPS.

The Teacher: For what? To know where they park the car and bury him.

Octello: It was a good game. Sorry, we couldn't do more for him.

The Teacher: Absolutely! Just be glad your man got this far.

Str8nger: He's not gone yet, guys.

The Teacher: Well, I'm hungry. Keep me posted so I can know when to collect.

Octello: Take a break Str8nger. We've been at this for days.

Str8nger: He's not done yet...

The Teacher: You're going to keep your hopes up and get your heart broken.

Str8nger: He's not done yet!

The Teacher: Okay...

§

Haven's first concern was figuring out where he was. At the turn off of I-35S, he saw the US-57S sign. Keeping an even more watchful eye, he was able to learn that he was heading toward Piedras Negras. It was a long stretch of road with farmland on either side. He had no idea why they were going this way, but he could imagine the worst. His immediate future had either an open field in it or some of that desert land that existed only about another hundred miles or so up the road. Either way, his final destination was going to be somewhere that would be hard to find if anyone at all cared to try to look.

He knew he had to think fast and the first thing was how to get out of his zip ties. Haven looked at his hands and figured out a plan, but he had to think the rest of it through. If he got his hands free, he was going to have to attack quickly. But who first? And how?

He thought of only one way any of it could work and then, he went for it. He leaned forward and grunted like he was passing out. Rip looked back and shook his head. He had plans for Haven when they got to the desert, but it looked like the man was probably not going to make it alive. He was going to have to dig the man's grave for him instead of having Haven do it himself.

When Rip turned back around, Haven immediately sprung into action. In one swift motion, he used his knee to break the zip tie. It worked like a charm and it was done in an instant. Before Rip had a chance to know what was going on, his vision flashed to white light and he could only feel immense pain.

Haven had grabbed Rip's head and pushed his eyes through his eye sockets with his fingers. Ripping outward, Haven broke the zygomatic bones on both sides of Rip's skull. It happened so fast, Art was busy keeping the SUV on the road while fumbling for his gun. When he finally pulled it out, Haven grabbed his arm and twisted it around the back of the seat.

The vehicle swerved and Art lost control. In mere seconds, the SUV was rolling through a ditch. It came to a stop upside down. Haven had taken a beating in the back seat and found himself on the ceiling with Art's arm still in his hand, the gun safely pointing away.

When Art came to, it was a second later. He looked over and saw that Rip was trying to say something, but he couldn't make it out. It was just a bunch of gibberish and then, he saw why. A steel signpost was sticking out of his ribs. Art looked back and saw Haven staring back at him. It was as if they were both out of it, but in a race to see who could come back to their senses first.

Art's arm was extremely dislocated. Haven didn't have to fight to get the gun free. Art's hand opened voluntarily, but he reached back with his other hand and tried to fight for his gun. A short struggle ensued and Art's lights went completely out. When the gun went off, the bullet went through Art's hand first and then through his face.

Haven kicked open the window and climbed out. He stumbled a little as he climbed out of the ditch and got back up to the road. When he pulled his phone out of his pocket, he looked at it in astonishment, "This would make a great commercial."

His phone was fine. Not a scratch on it. But it didn't have service. That's how far out in the middle of nowhere he was. All he could hope for was a car coming through. So, he looked at the upside-down vehicle and thought of anything he might need. A change of shirt would be a good idea. The blood might be alarming to anyone who saw him, but that was it. He looked at the gun in one hand and his phone in the other.

He put the gun in his cargo pocket and reached back for his wallet. When he was sure it was there, he looked up and down the empty road. With everything he needed and nothing more, he started walking back the way he had just come. His laptop and his clothes were in the SUV, but he couldn't carry them. He'd just have to clean up this mess later. His daughter was too important, more important than anything else.

He didn't let the dire details of his situation get to him. He didn't try to think about how far away his daughter might be at this point or how he was ever going to catch up to her. He just started walking. As long as he had breath and as long as he had strength, he had hope.

§

A man in khaki cargo pants and a black polo with the yellow letters "FBI" proudly displayed on the left side of his chest walked down the hallway at F.B.I. Headquarters, Washington D.C. He stopped at an office and looked in where an agent was rummaging through paperwork at his desk.

The agent at the door waited a moment and then, he spoke, "Daschel!"

When the agent looked up from his desk, he answered, "Trudy. What uh, what's up?"

Agent Trudy cocked his head, "Do we have a case with Haven Kayd?"

"With who," Agent Daschel responded, and then it hit him, "Oh, the kidnapping. No. There's a case to find her, but we don't have a case at all with him."

"Are you sure," Trudy pushed.

"Uh, yeah. Why," Daschel asked.

"The news," Trudy answered, "It's in the paper." Trudy held up a copy of the *Washington Daily*.

"Oh yeah," Daschel said knowingly, "You know the news. That's the news for you."

"This is the *Washington Daily* though," Trudy pointed out, "It's not a rag about women getting pregnant from aliens and stuff like that."

Daschel stared at Trudy for a moment, "There's no case."

Trudy nodded and then knocked on the door as he backed away, "Okay."

§

Haven had been walking for about two hours and had made it nearly eight miles when his wish finally came true. He could hear the sound of a car engine coming his way. So, he turned around to wave it down. To his surprise, the car slowed down and came to a halt.

Haven looked in the open window, "I need a ride."

The driver, a very young man looked back at him, "I can see that. Get in."

Haven got in the passenger seat, but the car didn't move. When Haven looked over at the driver, he was staring back at him, "Do you want to go back and get your stuff?"

"What," Haven asked.

"That is your car back there a few miles," the man asked.

Haven thought fast, "I need to get to where I can make phone calls and get that towed. I'll get my stuff then."

"Good enough," the driver said as he stepped on the gas, "My name's Kris by the way."

Haven shook his head slowly trying to stall while he came up with something to say, "I'm Jim."

Kris nodded, "Jim? Nice to meet you, Jim," he said with slight hesitation. He drove for a minute in silence and then, he broke, "There's this guy they call The Captain. Have you heard of him?"

Haven looked over at Kris with suspicion, "No."

"You've never heard of him," Kris nodded, "Well, his daughter was kidnapped and it's all over the internet. Are you sure you never heard about that?"

Haven nodded and then he couldn't believe what he was about to do. The man in the driver's seat was so young, too young to be dragged into this. But he grabbed his gun as fast as he could, "Who are you?"

"Hey," Kris kept both hands on the wheel, but his eyes grew wide, "I'm just trying to help, man."

"Look! I don't know who you are," Haven yelled, "But all I need is to get to a rental and that's all I need. I don't need a hard time."

"Yeah, yeah. That all sounds good," Kris responded, "I'll get you to a rental. I'll drive you there."

Haven hesitated, "Okay. I don't want anything else. I don't need any trouble."

"Yeah. That's fine," Kris confirmed.

"Okay," Haven said as his tone started to calm down.

Kris looked over at Haven and then down at the gun, "You can put that away. I know I'm a stranger, but I'm a fan. I've been following the story."

Haven looked at the kid and then at his gun. With a nod, he dropped the gun, but he kept it on his lap, "Just in case you want to try anything."

Kris nodded, "Man, I'm on your side Captain. I know what you're going through."

"You do," Haven asked.

"They've put you through a lot and they keep putting you through more. I don't know how anyone could *NOT* be on your side."

Haven coughed as he stared straight forward. For the first time in a few days, he had a moment to reflect. What he was up against was a little overwhelming. It started to circle his brain until he shook it off. He didn't have time to deal with those thoughts. He didn't need them dragging him down.

That's about the time he could hear Kris still talking, "But when I heard the story about you going down in Afghanistan and spending years in the POW camp, that was something right there. I can't imagine what that would be like. And then when they just up and abandoned you in there, how is that? How does something like that even happen? I don't know about you, but that would have freaked me out..."

Haven saw the gas station where they had turned off of I-35S, "Here! We can do this here." Haven was pointing at the gas station.

"Are you sure," Kris asked.

"Yes, right here," Haven confirmed, "I'll just call them and have them bring me a rental."

"They do that," Kris asked in amazement.

"Yes, they do that," Haven answered.

"Oh yeah, I forgot who I'm talking to," Kris reminded himself, "I'm talking to The Captain. Of course, they'll bring you a rental."

Kris pulled into the gas station and Haven couldn't get out quick enough. Kris was a nice enough kid, but he kept talking about things. Those things cut Haven deep. He was on a mission to save his daughter or he'd still be dealing with all the scandal that got him in this situation in the first place.

"Do you need anything like gas or something," Haven offered to thank Kris for giving him a ride.

"No," the young man answered, "I just hope you find her."

"Thanks, man," Haven said as he nodded, "Hope so."

Kris nodded back and then drove away while Haven pulled his phone out of his pocket. He looked at his phone with a slight smile on his face. He had service.

After putting in an order for a car, Haven went to his Facebook page and started typing, "I'm not out of the game yet!"

Chapter XIV

"You can't drive down the road looking through the rearview mirror."

Str8nger: Looks like you owe me Teach.

The Teacher: This guy has become my real hero.

Octello: I might have to introduce myself to him one day.

Str8nger: Getting a crush on him?

Octello: Could be. Yeah, I think I am.

§

By the time his rental was delivered to him, Haven knew where his daughter was and what direction he needed to go. Str8nger even put to rest any worries Haven might have had by sending him a screen capture of Lara in the car at a light. That put his mind at ease somewhat as he headed North on US-285 on his way back to I-10.

Even though he had to make up for some lost time, he knew he needed to take care of something else first. He had to visit a pharmacy and get some proper medical attention to his bullet wound. He figured if he found a Walmart, he could get in and out without anyone noticing or even caring to notice him. Plus, he'd be able to grab a few extra things he needed and get back on the road.

Thankful for self-checkout lines, Haven was in and out without incident. A lady wearing her nightgown wasn't paying attention to anyone. A guy in high heels and a cowboy hat had too much going on to worry about anyone else. Walmarts are safe places to hide. Those people are literally in their own world.

Trying to rush, Haven climbed in his car, took off his shirt, and laid over the center console to make his side a flat surface. Haven ripped open a quick clotting agent and poured it on the bullet wound. Then, he tore open a package of gauze to cover it. With absolutely no care in the world, Haven finally taped up the gauze with two long strips that formed an X over the wound. He knew that wasn't the best way to do it, but it was the fastest and that's all he cared about. He was back on the road in a matter of minutes and burning up the highway as fast as he could.

§

"Mr. President, it's a more serious matter than all these conspiracy theories circling the internet," George's White House Chief of Staff, Tom Monahan, was sitting in a chair in front of the President's desk in the Oval Office.

George looked around at the several people in on this conference. Beside Tom was Trey Booker, the Director of National Intelligence, as well as Ben Crowell, the Director of the FBI, and Paul Bowen, the Deputy Director of the FBI. Four men in suits and greying haircuts that screamed they were all mere photocopies of each other. George couldn't believe what he was hearing, "This is what we're talking about? This is why all of you have come here today? Look around this room. Look at the four of you. We're talking about a missing child and this Captain Haven Kayd guy? Don't get me wrong. I want that child found. But there are what, thousands of missing children, hundreds of thousands of missing children? Why is this one so special, it calls for a conference with the four of you in my office?"

"Mr. President," Trey responded, "It wasn't on our radar at first, but there is a deeper matter here. Haven Kayd makes assertions on his site that the scandal involves human trafficking and a shell company to funnel money through."

George cocked his head as he shook it back and forth, "This guy has a blog. It's a blog and you guys are reading it, believing everything you're reading?"

Ben nodded, "It checks out."

George's head shook in shock as his eyes went wide, "It checks out?"

Trey grunted a heavy sigh, "We've come across some information that this is all true."

George took another moment to look around, "And you're saying this is in our own backyard?"

Paul shifted in his seat, "We have intercepted messages from code name Baroness Coutts. Our records indicate that she originally orchestrated a new military contract years ago and has been running the operations since."

"So, what you're trying to say," George said heatedly, "Is that our military is involved in human trafficking?"

"Uh, no sir," Tom shook his head adamantly, "A government contract has been used to funnel the money through. The acting agents are not military."

"Not military," George repeated, "Who's Baroness Cou…"

"Coutts," Paul assisted.

"Coutts," George continued, "Who is she?"

"We do not know that, yet," Trey answered.

"Well, what's it going to take," George asked.

All the men looked around at each other. Then, Ben answered, "We'll dedicate a special team to it, sir."

"Is that double talk," George asked earnestly, "Like, you'll form a committee to study if you need to form a committee?"

"Uh, no sir," Ben answered, "We'll find her."

"Let me say this in no unclear words," George started.

"Yes sir," the four men said in unison.

"I want this whole thing taken down. Dismantled, gutted from the inside out," George ordered.

The four men nodded together, "Yes sir!"

§

A small town known as Truth or Consequences, New Mexico sits along I-25N. A peaceful town that is home to just over six thousand people. It's a great place to enjoy a nice quiet vacation or to hide your business if you have business worth hiding.

Haven followed his phone. He had learned to trust the hidden guys behind their keyboards. What other choice did he have? They had gotten him this far and they had not been wrong once. How they did what they did, he didn't know. But he was thankful.

Haven was encouraged further by the fact that he knew he only had one person to go up against. He knew where the other two were and they weren't going to be joining the party any time soon. That left one man standing, albeit the one with special forces training. Haven was going to have to be very smart about every move he made.

Haven's GPS led him through the small town of Truth or Consequences and then, it kept going. He found himself eventually turning off the highway and driving along a two-lane road where he passed a small airport getting ever closer to his destination. Another turn and it looked like he'd be there.

His GPS took him a few more miles and indicated that his destination was on the right. Haven slowed the car down and looked. There was an old, dilapidated diner in the middle of barren desert land. He grabbed the binoculars and took a closer look at the situation. There were two vehicles, Henry's and another one he couldn't identify, a black Lexus. He knew he had found the place. His daughter was there.

He looked around as good as he could and he found no one outside. So, Haven drove up the road a little further, and then cut across where there was no road so that he could come up behind the diner and get into an advantageous spot. He drove slow and steady so as not to kick up any dust. Stealth was key and he was doing the best he could.

§

Back at the J. Edgar Hoover Building in Washington, D.C., Agent Daschel stood at Agent Trudy's door. Trudy had no idea he was there until Daschel knocked. His head snapped up, "You again. What's going on?"

"I thought you said we didn't have anything going on with Captain Kayd," Daschel asked.

Trudy cocked his head in confusion, "What uh, what?"

"Guys left earlier today. They are on their way to New Mexico. Shouldn't we have been briefed," Daschel informed.

Trudy looked at his laptop and started typing. When he pulled it up, he nodded in recognition, "It looks like a special emergency team coordinated earlier today from El Paso. We weren't invited."

"What's going on," Daschel asked with a hint of attitude, "Are we going after this guy or not?"

Trudy looked at the laptop and then shook his head as he looked back at Daschel, "You know as much as I do."

From a distance, a low rumble of rotors could be heard getting ever closer. Two ominous silhouettes suddenly appeared on the blue and orange horizon. They came low and they came fast from the South.

When the Black Hawks landed at the Truth or Consequences Municipal Airport, heavily armed men from the Hostage Rescue Team jumped out and started directing the UH-60s into empty hangars. The doors were quickly closed and the teams swiftly swept the area.

Using only hand signals to communicate, the teams coordinated their efforts and took cover in different locations between the hangars. They could easily see in all directions and with a thumbs up, they were ready. One team started movement across the desert while the other took cover in a hangar. All they needed now was for the right visitors to come along at the wrong time.

§

Haven was watching an older version of himself as he sat waiting patiently at the airport. He looked around confused and wondered why he was there. But more importantly, why was he watching himself. His older self looked excited and worried at the same time as he rubbed his sweaty palms on his legs and kept looking toward a certain gate.

It was a big airport that Haven was sure he had seen before. It was very familiar, but he couldn't remember which one it was. He had seen hundreds of airports throughout his pilot life. They all seemed to blend together even though they were each distinct.

Who was he waiting for? Why was he there? As he watched himself patiently waiting, he started to feel what the old man was feeling. A lonely man who was waiting for someone special. A man with a smile on his face, but a frown on his soul. Haven suddenly became deeply concerned.

He looked toward the gate and then back at himself. When the door opened, it took a moment for people to start coming up the ramp. The old man stood up with a slight stiffness in his hip and started looking around excitedly. Haven looked back and forth as he watched himself get excited when people started walking through the door, but they passed the old man like he wasn't even there.

They kept coming and coming, but no one looked familiar. The old man was looking at each and every one of them. But eventually, the last person stepped off the plane. The old man looked around confused, and then he looked back at the door as if someone else was going to magically appear.

Haven's heart dropped. He felt the pain the old man was feeling. She didn't come. Haven was picking up on the emotion his older self was feeling. She didn't promise him that she would. He was just hoping and his hope was empty. His daughter didn't get on the plane. She hadn't come to see him.

Suddenly, Haven jerked out of his deep sleep. He looked around confused for a moment but quickly caught his senses. He was at the diner and both cars were still there. He looked at his phone for the time to calculate that he had only drifted off for about ten minutes.

He shook himself awake. He couldn't afford to fall asleep no matter how tired he was. He had to be alert and ready for anything. He had no idea how he was going to save his daughter or what it was going to take, but he had to be ready for anything.

Then, he saw movement. Two men left the diner and got in the Lexus. Lara wasn't with them. It was just those two men. Haven's car was strategically parked on the side of the building in the shade. He could see the entrance road from where he was, but he was confident that he was well hidden from their view.

As he watched the men get in the car and drive out the other way, Haven figured Lara was still inside with Henry. So, he checked his gun and made sure it was loaded. Then, he bowed his head and sucked in a deep breath. He built up his motivation, and then he went on the move.

Chapter XV

"If you have to lie to make your point, you don't have a point."

Sitting at her desk, Sarah couldn't believe what she was reading. Captain Kayd's website was at it again. It wasn't enough for him that his daughter had been kidnapped and as of just a few moments ago had been sold for a very lofty price, but he was asking for even more repercussions. Sarah shook her head as she said to herself, "He must be out of his mind."

Captain Kayd Online

"Exposed: How High Does The Human Trafficking Ring Go?"

You've followed the scandal from day one and you probably couldn't believe what you were reading at times. Trust me! Neither could we. The Captain's name has been dragged through the mud and they've put him through the worst that can be imagined.

Kidnapping his daughter was an all-time low, but that's about to be resolved as we speak. You'll get the update as soon as we have it. But, you know you've been waiting on this bit of information. How high does this scandal go? You'd be surprised.

Confidential documents that have been leaked to us by credible sources indicate that the scandal goes all the way up to the...

Sarah grabbed her phone and sent out a message as fast as she could type when she was suddenly startled by a familiar voice behind her, "So, you're the Baroness?"

She turned around to find her husband standing behind her, "How long have you been standing there?"

"Long enough," George answered as he walked around the room, "I have the FBI trying to figure out who the Baroness is and she's right under my nose. That's a clever name by the way. Baroness Coutts, a lady who gave homes to the poor. I should have known from the name. Your work is to give homes to the homeless. But here you are, taking kids from their homes."

Sarah looked at him with thoughts running through her mind. She could deny everything, but would that do any good? She was caught. There was no way out of it. She decided to simply explain, "George, I didn't want to be involved in this. I didn't want to be any part of that. You have to believe me."

"How does that work," George asked, "That you got involved in it then?"

"I signed for the shell company without knowing what was really behind it," Sarah started to explain, "By the time I realized what was really going on, I was in too deep. They held it over my head. They wouldn't let me back out of it."

"When was this," George asked confused.

"When I was a senator," she answered timidly.

"But now," after thinking it through, the President went on, "You're orchestrating the worst parts of it. You had an innocent man's daughter kidnapped. How do you justify getting tricked into it and now becoming the worst part of it?"

"It's a house of cards," she answered, "If one card falls, the whole house caves in. I can't take that. I can't let it ruin my work or your work. I can't let it put a stain on your presidency."

"My presidency," George fired back, "My presidency won't take a hit. Do you hear me? Your hands are dirty, not mine."

Sarah had no idea what her husband was capable of doing. She had no idea what was going through his mind at the moment. Could he turn against her? Would he? She never fathomed that she would ever see that day, but she was about to find out. She could see the steam coming off his neck. She could clearly see he was upset, but she had never seen him this upset.

He walked to the window with his hands on his hips, and then he looked back at her. He studied her face and saw the fear in her eyes. Her life was in his hands at the moment and for some reason, that's what she feared the most.

"Okay," he started, "I have FBI in New Mexico. They think they know where the girl is. At least, I hope they know where the girl is. You're going to make sure they are right. Then, we'll bring her and him back home. We win. We're out. I take this whole thing down and that becomes the defining moment of my presidency."

"You're going to get me out," Sarah asked in surprise.

He shook his head and studied her for a moment. It was as if she had no idea who he was, "What kind of husband would I be if I didn't stand by your side?"

Sarah looked at him like she had never loved him as much as she did at that moment, "What about the accusation he makes about me being involved?"

"Don't worry about that," he boasted with pride, "It's so easy to get people to believe anything."

Sarah's face lit up with a look of relief. She could drop the weight off her shoulders finally. It felt so good. At that moment she forgot about everything else going on in her life, especially the message on her phone that had already been sent.

§

Within the hour, Haven's Facebook was taken down due to violating "community standards." Don't think that didn't get noticed in the underground world where his fans lingered, and his articles were being shared. They made a big deal about it across their own profiles, but the big cog that makes the machine work didn't budge. Protests fell on deaf ears.

So, the huge network of fans started sharing Captain Kayd's articles everywhere. They weren't going away. Fact-checkers disputed any claims that were made. An algorithm was put in place to search for and identify any article shared on Facebook from *Captain Kayd Online*. Wherever they were, what soon appeared was the message, "Content No Longer Available."

The fans wrote about what was going on in their forums and chat rooms. They knew The Captain was under attack and now they knew how high it went. That was the one thing about The Captain's site. Facebook could take down his profile, but no one could touch his site. The web hosting company wasn't as easy to work with as Facebook had been.

It didn't matter if his site was a little harder to take down than his Facebook profile. It was a blog, a blog written by a man with a limited perspective. When the dust settled and his daughter was safe, he would see it their way. The President himself and the First Lady took it upon themselves to save her life. How could they be a part of human trafficking when they went out of their way to save her and dismantle the entire system that put her in danger in the first place?

That was how they reasoned with themselves. In their experience, it had worked that way in the past many, many times. People were easy to manipulate. They were easy to control. What would make this situation any different?

Chapter XVI

"As long as the pieces kept falling, I kept going."

Henry was looking at his account on his phone and counting the zeroes when he saw something move out of the corner of his eye. He looked at the windows, and then he looked around the room. He must have just been seeing things.

That's when he heard a ding on his phone. It was from the Baroness, "I want him dead!" Henry nodded with a grin across his face. He was about to get paid again. This was going to turn out to be a great month.

Haven was hiding between the windows, a fully loaded gun in hand. He had squatted underneath each one as he made his way toward the door. He had one window to go and as he made his move, Henry saw him.

Haven could hear the gunfire and watched as the window exploded next to him. He turned toward the door and kicked it open, and then he dropped down as he came inside and hid behind the first booth.

"Captain," Henry yelled, "You're too late!"

"Where is she," Haven yelled back.

"Not here," Henry laughed as he stood in the middle of the diner, defiant.

"Where is she, Hank," Haven asked with attitude.

"Probably on her way to Brazil or Argentina by now," Henry answered.

Haven quickly rose and took a shot over the booth. It missed Henry, but he knew it was time to take cover. He jumped behind the counter.

Haven glimpsed a view of Henry in the mirror. So, he ran bent over to the counter himself. Then, he yelled, "Lara! Lara!"

"I just told you," Henry said, "She's not here."

"You'll have to understand if I don't believe you," Haven responded.

"You know, I do have a lot of respect for you Captain," Henry thought he'd take the moment to say, "Even if I have to kill you."

Haven glimpsed another view of Henry through the mirror to make sure he wasn't getting any closer, "Oh yeah? Why's that?"

Henry had his back against the counter and he could see the mirror, but he didn't have the advantage Haven had. All Henry could do was rely on hearing Haven's voice to be able to tell where he was, "I don't know of anyone who would have come after their daughter the way you did. It's a shame."

"What's a shame," Haven answered, "The fight isn't over."

"Oh, it's over," Henry laughed, "And I owe you." Henry felt the back of his head, "I still have a nice knot."

"Well, you shot me," Haven informed, "So, I'd say we're even."

Henry laughed more, "See? I think we would have been friends in another life."

In an instant, Haven jumped around the corner of the counter and took his shot. Henry was quick to move, but Haven's bullet got him in the leg.

He looked in the mirror and saw that Henry had slipped on the floor and seemed to be lying still. That was his moment. He rushed out from behind the counter to get a better shot, but that's where he met Henry's bullet. Henry heard him coming and rolled over on his side to take the shot.

Haven landed on the floor sitting up with a bullet hole in his chest. He looked at Henry with no expression as his thoughts raced with memories of his daughter. Swimming in the lake and teaching her to float. Seeing her face as he presented her with a dollhouse he had labored over with love. Empty memories because he hadn't actually done those things with her. They were creatively constructed in his mind while he was in the POW camp. His soul went dark and his thoughts suddenly came back to reality.

As Haven's back hit the floor, Henry struggled to get to his feet. Haven could hear the scraping of a foot as Henry got closer and closer to him. He could feel the man standing above him and when he looked, Henry had his pistol aimed at his head.

In an instant, Haven raised his gun and fired. Henry stood there for a moment, and then his legs went weak. He stumbled backward and fell to the ground with a bullet hole in his forehead.

The HRT Unit finally reached the diner. They had heard the gunshot, a weird sound that seemed to echo as if two shots were fired at the same time. When they entered the diner, their thoughts were confirmed.

Two men were lying on the ground. Both had been shot in the head by the last shots they would ever take. The Lead Agent radioed it in as he kicked the gun out of Haven's hand, and then walked over and kicked the gun out of Henry's hand.

As he stood over Haven's body, he shook his head in pity, "Well Captain, we'll get your daughter for you. Don't you worry about that."

He looked up at the agents at the door. One just shook his head as he looked down at Haven while the other made the sign of the cross over his heart.

§

The black Lexus drove up a side road along the flight line. Then, it pulled in front of an empty hangar. Both of the men got out of the car, but only one started toward the door.

Then, he looked back, "Sal! Sal!"

Sal turned his head, "What?"

"You're not coming in," the man asked in return.

Sal completely turned around and looked his friend square in the eye, "Ravi, if you can't handle a little girl by yourself, I don't know if I want to work with you anymore."

Ravi waved his hand in Sal's direction and then went inside the hangar. As soon as Sal was all by himself, three HRT agents rushed him before he had a chance to react. They arrested him with no incident and swiftly moved him to a safe area away from the car.

Inside, Ravi walked across the empty floor, his shoes clicking and echoing off the walls. Lara could hear him coming and she tried to struggle out of her cuffs. She was locked in an office with her hands cuffed to a pipe above her head and her mouth was taped.

When Ravi looked in the window, he shook his head and unlocked the door. As he approached her, he said to her, "I don't know why they do this. We're in the middle of nowhere. No one can hear you."

He pulled the tape off her mouth and then he uncuffed one hand as he turned her away from him and cuffed her again behind her back. She eyed him while holding back the tears.

"My dad's coming, you know," she said, "He'll find you."

As Ravi walked her out of the office, "Hate to tell you, kid. But the last I heard, he was on his way to Mexico. He's probably in his grave by now."

Her eyes grew wide and then red as tears started to flow. Ravi walked her across the hangar floor and out the door where he found the car surrounded by the HRT. He turned to pull Lara back into the hangar, but he was met with an HK416 in his face.

When Lara realized she was safe, she started asking, "Where's my dad? Do you guys know? Does anyone know where my dad is?"

Her questions were met with silence. Of course, they knew. But who knew how to tell a young lady the bad news?

§

George entered the bedroom and found Sarah sitting at the desk. With his hands on his hips, he nodded, "They got the girl, but he didn't make it."

Sarah looked at him confused, "He didn't make it?"

"No," George confirmed, "He was killed in a diner by your guy. Don't worry about him though. The Captain got the best of him too."

"He didn't make it," Sarah repeated herself, and then she looked at her laptop with that same look of confusion on her face.

Captain Kayd Online

"The Final Update"

Just so you know, The Captain took his last breath earlier today at an abandoned diner on the outskirts of Truth or Consequences, New Mexico. It served as a hub for human trafficking and he was able to track his daughter's kidnappers down to that spot.

Actually, there was only one kidnapper standing by that time. The Captain had taken out two of them already when they were trying to take him to Mexico and bury him in the desert. But The Captain had a completely different idea about that as he managed to take control of the situation. We wish we had more details. We're sure this will all eventually come out.

We are happy to report that his daughter is safe. She was rescued by a highly trained FBI Team, but questions linger. If that's what it was going to take, why weren't they sent earlier? We'll follow up with that and hopefully, we can get some answers...

Chapter XVII

"When you give your life to something, it would be nice to know it was worth giving your life for."

As George walked up to the presidential podium on the South Lawn, he looked out at all the cameras in his face as well as the people in attendance. His intel informed him that the three people involved in the kidnapping were all deceased so Sarah was safe from that scandal and he was free to talk about it any way he wished, "The FBI acted on an anonymous tip and expertly executed a rescue mission to bring Lara Kayd home safe to her mother."

George held out his hand gesturing to Monica, Skip, and Lara sitting in the audience. Then, a somber expression came over the President's face as he continued, "Sadly, Captain Haven Kayd became a casualty in his own war. He was a brave man who served his country proudly. It is a sad case indeed that he is no longer with us. We will always consider him one of our country's great treasures..."

As the President continued in his speech, Lara's imagination drifted. She remembered those moments when she was a child and she would think about her father as if he was there. It made her feel empty and alone inside, but also as if he was still with her if you can imagine that strange mix of emotion. She held onto that because she didn't want to lose him again. She wasn't ready for that just yet. She felt so strongly that at any minute, he was going to walk across the White House lawn, and there he'd be. Sadly, that never happened. He was truly gone. She would have to eventually come to terms with that.

§

In the days that followed, Lara was put through a lot. She was followed by cameras and she was called by journalists who wanted an exclusive story. Of course, the President made sure to debrief her first. He made sure to do that before she agreed to do any interviews.

The President's team showed Lara the evidence that they had and made sure she understood their side of the truth. A truth that wasn't very true at all. But he who holds the information controls the narrative. Lara had no idea what she had actually been through and it wasn't hard for her to get turned around on it.

The demand was too great, and Monica finally agreed to one exclusive television interview to set the record straight and hopefully, Lara would be able to put it all behind her. If one thing Monica knew, Lara hadn't quite mourned the death of her father yet. No one was giving her the time. Everyone wanted to ask those probing questions that did more to cut deep into her emotions than to help her get past it.

If anything, giving one television program an exclusive interview would squash the bloodthirst and the interest in Lara's story would fade. The vultures would quit picking and fly away. So, the interview was set and Monica made sure to get Lara to the station. In fact, she did it in style. She rented a limo for the occasion.

Sitting in front of Shera Goodwin, the host of *American Times*, Lara felt a little intimidated. She looked at the camera and all the lights in front of her. She knew Shera was there, but she could hardly see with the bright lights in her face.

"Are you ready," Lara heard Shera ask.

"Uh, yes," Lara answered with slight hesitation.

"Okay, I'm just going to start asking you a few questions, and then we'll put the interview together later in the editing room," Shera informed, "That makes it so that this is relaxed and you don't have to worry about making mistakes. Just start over or keep talking, whatever works for you. Okay?"

"Okay," Lara nodded.

"Lara, you were recently kidnapped by human traffickers," Shera began, "What was that like?"

Lara furled her eyebrows as she looked back at Shera with a slightly confused look on her face, "Um, they weren't human traffickers. They were actually trying to save me."

Shera stirred in her seat, "Uh, what? They were trying to save you?"

Lara looked around at all the silhouettes that she could see around the room, "Uh yes, that's what I was told in one of my briefings. My dad was suffering from a mental breakdown and he thought I had been kidnapped. But he had become very dangerous. So, those men were trying to save me from him."

Shera shook her head in full disbelief. She couldn't believe what she was hearing, "Weren't you handcuffed? Didn't they find you in an office in a hanger handcuffed to a pipe?"

"Um, I don't remember everything," Lara answered, "It all happened so fast and I was assigned a therapist. A really good therapist who said that some of the things are just part of my active imagination."

Shera looked through her notes and looked around at the producer who could only shrug. The host looked back at Lara, "Can you tell us what you do know?"

Lara adjusted in her seat and was hesitant to talk badly of her father. But she was only trying to tell the truth, "Well as I said, he was suffering from a mental breakdown. I read some headlines in the newspapers that talked about that. He was a POW and he had really been through a lot over there. It did something to him. When he came back, he thought he was still over there. And it got real bad. He killed those guys, the guys he thought kidnapped me. He killed them. That's what it was doing to his brain. They said it was PTSD or something. The things he was writing on his website show how far gone his mind was, but he taught me something about that. He taught me about lying. He taught me when I tell a lie, to tell the lie close to the truth. That way, it's easier to keep the details straight. I guess that's what made it make sense to everyone. It's so easy to get people to believe anything you want them to. I guess he started to believe those things himself."

With her mind totally blown, Shera kept pressing for details from her notes and Lara kept answering. The interview went on for about thirty minutes, and then Shera wrapped it up, "Well Lara, I would like to thank you for being so candid in this interview. I can't imagine going through what you went through and I'm sorry that you lost your father...again."

Lara nodded, but she didn't say anything. She simply stared back at Shera while patiently waiting to be excused. It was over. Hopefully, Lara could get back to a somewhat normal life and begin to heal.

As she and Monica made their way outside, the photographers swarmed them and followed them to the limo. Skip did his best to hold the door open and make a path, but one photographer broke through.

He shoved a note in Lara's pocket, "Here! Take this." Then, the photographer backed off and disappeared into the crowd.

Lara finally made it in the car where Monica pulled her close and comforted her. With tears coming to Lara's eyes, she reached for the note in her pocket. She opened it up and showed it to her mom, "My name is Casper. I knew your father. We need to talk. I'll be in touch."

Lara and Monica looked at each other. She turned the note over and there was nothing on the back. Then, she read it again as she held it in her lap.

As the limo drove away, a man watched from the distance. A silhouette in the shadow was all Lara could see as the limo rolled by and the man was eventually out of sight. She looked down at the note in her hand and wondered.

Book Connections

When You Miss Me

From Chapter VI

"Just close your eyes and I am there! It's never too long before we are...together again," Haven closed the pages he had been reading.

Those lines are from Michael Allen's *When You Miss Me*.

A River in the Ocean

The memories Lara and Haven share are the same imaginations shared between Krista and Chris in Michael Allen's *A River in the Ocean*.

Also from *A River in the* Ocean is the diner Haven visits when he travels through Fredericksburg, Virginia. Krista and Chris are sitting in the booth Haven is observing as he's eating breakfast.

Made in the USA
Columbia, SC
08 March 2021